Praise for *The Mystery of the Colour Thief*

'Helping a friend rescue an ailing cygnet offers
redemption in a poignant, beautifully poised tale.'
Financial Times, Books of the Year

'I'm lost for words! I thought taking on such a
sensitive subject matter was portrayed beautifully
and the parallels between colour and her
emotions was so clever.'
Grace Barrett, Waterstone's Bookseller, Ipswich

'This is a powerful story... about the rebuilding of
self-esteem and the blossoming of new friendships
and most importantly, the return of hope.'
The School Librarian

'Paints a convincing picture of a harrowing time
in a young life... offering ample humour,
hope and optimism.'
BookTrust, Book of the Month

'A really impressive, nuanced debut looking
at how to cope with and survive life.'
The Bookseller

'This extremely readable novel lays bare the
emotions of friendship and family, as well as
exploring the impact of nature on our urban lives,
and the ways in which we can find hope and
confidence in ourselves.'
Minerva Reads

'Powerful feelings are handled in a compassionate
way, characters are authentically nuanced
and the plot is compelling.'
Books for Topics

'A fantastic story inspired by life.'
Mr Ripley's Enchanted Books

'Moving and emotionally highly charged, this is
a haunting story that will stay with you long
after the last page is read.'
Parents in Touch

The Mystery of the Colour Thief

EWA JOZEFKOWICZ grew up in Ealing, and studied English Literature at UCL. She currently works in marketing, and lives in Highbury, north London, with her husband and twin girls.

THE
Mystery
OF THE
Colour
Thief

Ewa Jozefkowicz

ZEPHYR

First published in the UK by Zephyr,
an imprint of Head of Zeus, in 2018
This paperback edition published in the UK
in 2019 by Head of Zeus Ltd

9 7 5 3 1 2 4 6 8

A catalogue record for this book is available
from the British Library.

ISBN (PB): 9781786698957
ISBN (E): 9781786698933

Printed and bound by CPI Group (UK) Ltd,
Croydon, CR0 4YY

Head of Zeus Ltd
First Floor East
5–8 Hardwick Street
London EC1R 4RG
WWW.HEADOFZEUS.COM

To Magda and Julia

One

He came out of nowhere, a man in the smoke. He was nothing more than a shadow at first, a smudge of black in the grey. But as he loomed closer, he grew bigger, became more solid. My heart was a drum. He was shouting at me, but the sound bounced off my ears in eerie echoes. His long arms reached out. He was so close that I could smell him - a mix of sweat and burning rubber. He leaned in...

3.05 a.m.

The luminous figures stared back at me in the dark. The glow of a street lamp seeped through the wooden slats of my blinds. It was quiet. The man had gone. A nightmare. Though somewhere in the depths of my mind I knew that it was more than a nightmare.

That morning I was late getting ready because Milo

wouldn't come in from the garden. He'd been leaping around like a maniac, chasing a tiny vole that he'd found. Eventually I managed to get him indoors and I waited for my best friend, Lou, while grabbing scraps of breakfast. Dad had gone to work already, leaving me a note on the kitchen table:

Diz, see you after school. Have a good day x.

Lou usually arrived at 8.45 a.m. on the dot, so we didn't have to rush, but it was almost 8.50 a.m., and she wasn't here. She must have been running late herself and decided to go in on her own. I couldn't wait any longer.

I broke into a run as soon as I was outside. My feet hit the pavement in sync with the beating of my heart. The houses on either side of Gulliver Avenue shifted and swayed, and my ears ached inside from the sharp nip in the early autumn air. Clusters of people huddled at the bus stop passed me in a burst of charcoal greys, the white and black of offices and banks and traffic merged into a single, moving stream.

I ran and ran until I reached the finish line of the school gates, my arms propped against the railings, my chest ready to burst. The bell had gone. Even the usual crowds of sixth formers with their slouchy rucksacks and rolled-up blazer sleeves had disappeared inside. I walked into the empty entrance hall.

Lou saw me by the lockers and gave me a disapproving glance, not mentioning a word about why she hadn't come to mine. I'd got used to these glances over the last few weeks. Ever since we'd started Year Eight, she'd been acting as though she was a guru on everything from clothes to hair, music and even who to hang around with.

'Why are you always so last minute about everything? And look at you - what's with the stains on the skirt?' She shook her head. I ignored her. Lou's own skirt was far too short and I hadn't said anything about that. She'd hitched it up recently to expose her skinny knees. It was part of her new look, which included poker-straight hair and thick smudged lines on her eyelids.

'Come on, Izzy, hurry up!'

And before I could ask her why she hadn't called for me on the way to school, she turned on her heel and disappeared in the direction of our classroom. I stood there, thinking that any second she would turn around and wait for me. She didn't.

'Izzy, what are you still doing here?' Mr McKenzie sounded irritated. 'Daydreaming in the corridor? It's already gone 9.05 a.m.! Get a move on.'

We had double maths first with Mr Coruna who was, as always, striding backwards and forwards at the front of the classroom with a dazed expression on his face. He looked as though, in his thoughts, he was somewhere far better. I liked him a lot - he was kind and funny, even if he wasn't always great at explaining things.

Today, his classroom was horribly hot, and Jonah and Dave were sniggering about something in the corner. I would put money on them having turned up the radiators just for a laugh. It was exactly the sort of thing that they would find hilarious.

Someone dropped a book on the floor and Mr Coruna was brought back to reality. He started talking about the value of 'x', but because of the heat and the fact that I wasn't very interested in algebra, my fingers lost their grip, my pen began to slip and my eyes grew heavy. I rested my head in my hands and pressed my knuckles against my eyelids, thinking that the pressure might help me stay awake. Despite my best efforts, I found myself drifting - a silhouette appeared, the flicker of a shadow in a swirl of smoke... and then the awful crawling began in the pit of my stomach.

'Izzy! Oi... he's going to notice.'

Lou's prod jolted me awake.

'Can't believe you fell asleep. What's wrong with you?'

'I don't know... Lou?'

'What?'

Her eyebrows were raised and she looked annoyed but I carried on. I had to tell somebody.

When Mr Coruna turned to write something on the board, I whispered, 'I had the most horrible nightmare last night. One I never want to have again. There was a man... a shadow man. He was all black – I couldn't see his face or anything. He came out of a cloud of smoke and he was shouting at me... I was so scared.'

I expected her to be shocked, but she rolled her eyes again and I noticed flecks of mascara on her eyelids, like two miniature feathery fans.

'What are you banging on about now, Izzy?' she whispered back. 'You're such a weirdo. You've been so different ever since...'

She tailed off and had the decency to look guilty for a moment, before turning to her equations again.

Mr Coruna tapped me gently on the arm as I was walking out of the classroom at the end of the lesson.

'Izzy,' he said, 'I just want to tell you how sorry I am for what happened to you. I also wanted to let you know, as your head of year, that we're going to do everything we can to support you. I hope you feel you can come to me if you need help with managing homework or anything else. You know, of course, that we have Mrs Tomkinson, the school counsellor. If you wanted to arrange a visit to...'

'I'm all right,' I said abruptly and immediately felt bad. I knew he'd meant well.

'Thank you,' I managed finally, before shuffling off.

But I wasn't fine when I got back to our form room for our last lesson to find Frank the Skank sitting next to me, in Lou's usual seat. His dark fringe fell into his eyes, but I could see that he was trying to avoid my gaze.

'What are you doing here?' I asked him.

'She wanted to swap. I... I said I didn't mind,' he stammered, glancing over at Lou, who was settling herself into a seat at the front of the class, next to Jemima. He brushed his fringe out of his eyes still avoiding my gaze, taking ages picking up the pen he'd dropped on the floor.

The shock rolled over me in waves. Lou was also being careful not to look at me, but I knew she realised I'd just found out what she'd done. She and Jemima were hunched together, giggling, as they looked at something on Lou's iPad.

I sat on the edge of my seat. Surely it was a joke? A mean joke. Any second now, Lou would start laughing at me for being such a sucker and believing she'd do that to me. But when the bell went for the start of the lesson, she hadn't budged.

I thought of saying something to our form teacher, Mr McKenzie, though he didn't care where we sat, as long as we were quiet and got on with what we were supposed to be doing. Every time anybody bothered him, he'd say that he had 'bigger fish to fry' as if he were some celebrity seafood chef. At the start of the year I'd wished more than anything that we could have had Mrs Gilberton again, but she was teaching the new Year Sevens. I imagined her with them now, wearing one of her homemade dresses, probably getting them to read 'The Rime of the Ancient Mariner' in different voices. If she'd been here, she would have noticed straightaway that something was up and she'd ask to speak to me or to Lou at the end of the lesson. She always helped to sort things out quietly, without making a fuss.

Now we just had Mr McKenzie and his limericks, which I couldn't focus on no matter how hard I tried.

It was sad because I loved limericks – they were my favourite poems. I'd written a great one for Dad about a man who lived in a bucket. It made him chuckle for the first time in weeks and I felt like I'd won the jackpot. But today two things on my mind left no space for anything else. The first was the nightmare man and the second was Lou. We'd been friends since playschool. She wouldn't give up on me. Would she?

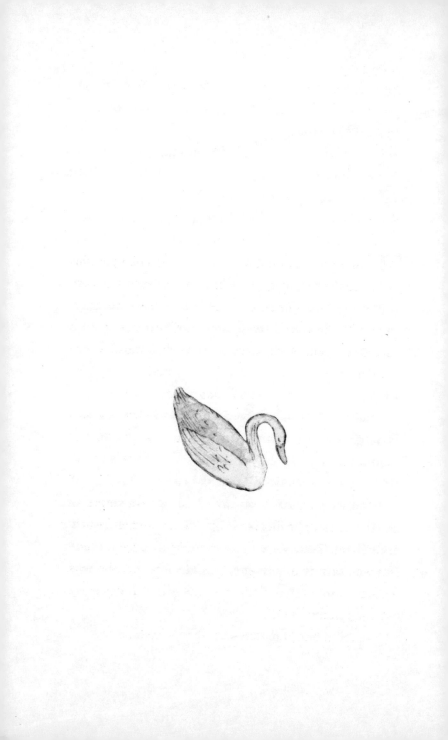

Two

That day, I got out of school as soon as I possibly could. Usually, Lou and I would walk together, but after what had happened, I was desperate to avoid her. I was walking so fast that I almost collided with some Year Sevens making their way to the tube station.

'Izzy?'

Drat. It was Lou's mum, Shelley. Of course – it was Monday, which meant she would be giving Lou a lift to swimming.

'Hi,' I said.

'How *are* you, Izzy?' she asked, her face arranged in an expression of concern. It struck me suddenly how unlike Lou she looked – she was all soft edges, where Lou was skinny and angular. I liked Shelley. She was the sort of mum that made even the worst things seem like they would be OK.

'I'm... I'm fine,' I muttered. 'I'm in a rush... I...'

9

But she continued to look at me and the more she looked, the more I felt her gaze piercing right through me.

'You haven't been to see us in a while,' she said. 'We miss you. You know you're always welcome.'

Of course I wasn't welcome. If only she knew... I opened and shut my mouth, feeling like an idiot. 'Thanks. I've just been very busy.'

'I know... I know, my love. Listen, I'm sure that many people will have said this to you, but if you ever need anything. Honestly, if you ever need anything at all, give me a call. Or you can just tell Lou, and she'll pass it on. Speaking of Lou... where is she?'

'Oh, she's still in class...' I hopelessly searched my brain for an excuse that would seem believable as to why I hadn't waited for her. I felt the heat rising inside me, and suddenly standing there in front of Shelley became unbearable. Out of the corner of my eye, I saw Lou and Jemima, listening to something on Lou's headphones, one ear-piece each.

'I have to go,' I told Shelley and was off before she had a chance to reply.

I stopped at the corner of Gulliver Avenue, where I knew that I was out of sight of them, and I leaned on a garden wall, breathing hard. I couldn't help looking back. From where I stood, I could make out Shelley trotting behind Jemima and Lou, trying to keep up. It was obvious that Lou hadn't told her anything – Shelley was just as clueless as I had been this morning. But Lou wouldn't have decided from one minute to another that she didn't want to be friends with me. She must have been thinking about it for a while... I carried on walking.

It was only when I turned into Ravens Road that I figured out where I was going. I hadn't intended to walk this way, but somehow my feet took me in the direction of the bus stop. The number eleven came within minutes, as if the driver knew I'd be waiting. Was it a sign?

A few sixth formers got on at the same time as me, but luckily one of my two favourite seats was free – on the top deck at the front. It was the seat Mum always sat me on, when I was small, because it had an amazing view and I could pretend that I was driving the bus.

'Mind that tree,' she used to say, as I held the imaginary steering wheel, and she'd shut her eyes in mock horror, as a particularly leafy one came our way. 'Phew, you got us past that – just.' I could hear her voice so clearly that if I closed my eyes, I really felt I was there. I could smell her perfume, sense the tickle of her long hair on my arm as she leaned close to hug me...

The driver hit the brakes, we were flung forwards, and the moment splintered. I moved to a different seat then - I couldn't bear the memory. One of the sixth form boys gave me a funny look, but I didn't care.

By the time I reached the hospital car park, it had started to rain. I walked to the main entrance through a cloud of fine, misty raindrops. It softened the edges of everything and calmed the scuttle-crawl in my stomach.

I knew where to go. Dad had made me memorise the route, so I could find my way easily if I came with Nanna Jem, Mum's mum, or someone else. 'It's the second floor in the lift, then follow the red arrows to Ward C.' He repeated the directions twice and smiled at me, but the smile didn't quite stretch to his eyes.

I hadn't made it very far yesterday, even though he was with me, or maybe *because* he was with me. Today I would do better. At the very least, I would step inside the room and look. I would have to look.

I worried for a second that somebody would stop me if I wasn't with Dad. But the nurse at the reception desk recognised me and nodded in the direction of the lifts.

That was it - no turning back. First the lifts, then the red arrows. I put my hand against my chest to calm the flutter, and turned the handle to the small room just off the side of Ward C.

There, wrapped up, pale and motionless, was my mum. It was her, of course it was her, but in many ways, it wasn't her at all. I dared myself to walk closer - one step, and then another. Her right arm lay over the covers, and there were tubes coming out of it. The other – the one that had been damaged – was carefully tucked away. The doctor had told Dad that he wasn't sure when they would try to bring her out of the coma. It depended on how she healed, but he was hopeful it would happen within a few weeks, so for now there was nothing to do except wait.

I saw that her hair had been cut, shorn close to her head. Something made me want to touch it – it was soft and suede-like. I thought I would feel angry that her long, dark brown curls had been reduced to this, but I felt no anger, there was just that same awful sting in the pit of my stomach. I had done this. It was all my fault. I had made her like this.

There were bruises on her left cheek and forehead, even though it had been five weeks and three days. They were shades of yellow and green.

My eyes followed their edges where they met the tiny veins beneath the surface of her skin at the temples.

'I'm sorry.' The words escaped my mouth before I realised I was saying them.

I reached to touch her, but at the last moment I snatched my hand back. I was frightened that Mum's would feel cold and lifeless – nothing like her usual firm, warm grip.

So I sat down in the grey, plastic chair and I talked to her. I talked to her for the first time since it happened.

'I'm having a horrible time without you. We all are. Lou is being strange. She doesn't want to be friends any more. She says I've changed since... since what happened. I don't think I have, but maybe?'

The whole day and more spilled out of me. I told Mum about the nightmare, and Lou making fun of my clothes, and the awful desk move.

I shut my eyes and wished more than anything that when I opened them, Mum would be turning around in bed, smiling at me, telling me not to worry about Lou - that things would be all right. She didn't. She lay there, still and quiet. The only sound was the occasional beep of the heart-monitoring machine with its zigzag on the screen. I had seen ones just like it on TV, and it seemed unreal that this particular one belonged to her. The beep grew louder and louder in my head, and then I was on my feet walking quickly out of the room.

'I'm sorry,' I whispered again, but nobody heard me.

Three

The beeping of the machine was still echoing in my head when I turned into our road, and I realised that I was scared of it. I knew it was a strange thing to be afraid of, because the beeping signified life. Maybe I was scared it would stop, as that's when you're really in trouble. It followed me, that beep - and I put my hands in my ears to try to make it go away. I walked like that all the way down the road but the sound continued, persistent and loud.

It only stopped when I spotted someone opposite our house - a small, silhouetted figure. At first I thought it might be a person sitting on a chair, which struck me as a strange thing to be doing in the middle of the pavement, but as I got closer, I saw it was a wheelchair.

In it sat a boy of about my age, with blond hair. A pair of round glasses balanced on his upturned nose. He grinned and waved. Just like that. It was the weirdest thing. Strangers hardly ever wave at each other. I didn't want to be rude so I waved back.

'Hi,' he said when I got within talking distance. He was smiling, a mysterious smile.

'Hi.'

'Does your head hurt?'

'What?'

'I saw you walking with your arms up...'

'Oh, right. No, it's nothing.'

He nodded. 'Are you in a hurry?'

I was - of course I was. I was always in a hurry. But to my surprise, I found myself saying, 'No, not really...'

'Can I show you something?'

'OK.'

'It's by the riverbank,' he said. The last of the sunlight reflected off his glasses and cast a glow over his face. I couldn't read his expression.

'Can I bring my dog?'

'Yeah, sure.'

He waited as I unlocked the door. Milo pelted out of the house, overjoyed, but he didn't jump on me as he usually did - he bundled himself straight into the lap of my new companion.

'Woah, woah.'

'Down, Milo, down. I'm so sorry. He's the most badly behaved dachshund in the world!'

But the boy somehow managed to calm Milo without losing control of the chair. Within moments, he was patting my dog's head and putting him back down on the ground. Milo ran circles around his new friend.

We made our way to the riverbank through the narrow gap between our house and the Lachmanns'. At first, the path was paved and even, so it was easy enough for the boy to wheel himself along, but then it turned to a muddy, stony track, and with every turn of the wheel, I thought he might slip and fall. My hands flew out several times, wanting to help, but he was always too quick for me and I noticed that there was something amazing about the way he held himself. His upper arms seemed incredibly strong, and with every judder over a stone or slippery patch, they brought him back into a steady forwards movement.

He stopped only when he was right at the edge of the water, and turned to grin again at me. Milo and I were a few metres behind, struggling to get through the mud. I hadn't been here since the spring and I'd forgotten how wet and boggy it could get. Every step was an effort.

'I'm Toby, by the way,' he said. 'I've moved into number thirty-two.'

'I'm Izzy. You moved into the abandoned house?'

'Yes, last week. It's a total mess inside, you know. Most things need replacing. Mum is only able to rent it because it's so cheap. I like it, though. I hope we can stay.'

'Why wouldn't you?'

'We need to find out whether Mum can get a permanent position at her work. That's why she hasn't signed me up for school yet. She's teaching me at home at the moment.'

'Nobody's lived there since old Mr Mason died...' I said, and then clamped my lips shut. He didn't need to know that. I knew I wouldn't want to, if I lived there.

But Toby wasn't listening. He was gazing at something in the middle of the river, his finger pressed against his lips.

'Just there. Be very quiet. Look.'

He spread apart the dense grass and pointed ahead. At first, I couldn't see what he wanted me to look at. My eyes scanned the murky water and the patches of bright green algae. A mist scurried across the river, making the hairs on the back of my neck stand to attention.

'Look closer. Just there.'

I peered at the other side of the bank. The water was moving fast, but the river itself wasn't wide. In the last glimmers of afternoon sunshine, I could make out leaves and twigs sticking up from under the surface. And then I saw them. On a branch, jutting from beneath a mulberry bush, was a group of small, awkward-looking grey cygnets gathered around their mother, their feathers shuddering in the breeze. There was something so fragile about them that it made me hold my breath.

'They're already a couple of months old,' Toby said. 'You can tell by their size and their soft feathers. I'm not sure where their dad is - I haven't seen him around. Look - there's a tiny one who can't quite keep up with the gang. You might not be able to see him because he's usually hiding behind the others, but you can recognise him by a funny tuft on his head. I called him Spike because of it.'

We edged closer to the bush, Milo pulling on his lead, itching to get into the water. I motioned for him to stay still. The mother swan's babies were all around her, swimming close together for warmth and safety. I counted four of them, alike in colour and size. Then I saw him - tucked between two branches that just skimmed the water, was Spike. His head was cocked comically to the side. He reminded me of an old man who's told a joke and is waiting for his audience's reaction. His brothers and sisters were ignoring him, busy trying to get their mother's attention.

'They're beautiful.'

'Yes.'

'And he's so delicate.'

'I think they hatched late, for cygnets. Usually they arrive earlier in the summer. That means they'll have more trouble finding food as it gets colder. And Spike's going to need help. We have to make sure that the others don't take it from him.'

I loved the way he said 'we'. It was as if the two of us and Milo were already a team. I felt a bond with Spike straightaway. He looked so tiny as he sheltered from the wind, but there was something determined about him. Every time it seemed that he was going to be left behind, he swam a little faster.

'Shall we come back tomorrow with some food for him?' I asked. 'We should probably get started with feeding him up as soon as possible.'

Toby shifted in his chair, the muscles of his shoulders tensing under his coat. Then he turned and looked at me, as if checking how serious I was about committing to Spike. I must have made a good impression, because he chose to reveal a secret.

'For sure. They'll be here for a while. And there's an old van there. We can hide out in it if it rains. The back door's missing, so I can wheel myself inside, if you give me a hand.'

He raised his eyebrow questioningly.

'Where?' I asked.

'On the other bank, behind the playground. Want to go over and see?'

It was getting dark. Tiny flickers from street lamps shone in the distance. I was just about to say that I had to head home, when my curiosity got the better of me. I tugged on Milo's lead and we followed Toby across the rickety wooden bridge. We went beyond the swings I used to twist myself around in when I was younger, and the broken seesaw covered in graffiti, and then Toby pointed to a clump of bushes which separated the playground from some wasteland.

'We need to get to the other side,' he said. I scoured for a space where the branches were sparser so that Toby could wheel himself through.

He was right about the van. It stood on the edge of the field, as if it had always been there, as if it was the most normal thing in the world. Even in the half-dark, I could see it was rusting. There were three words written on the side in bold, slanting letters. The first was obscured by a stuck-on piece of cardboard, but I was pretty sure that the other two read: *Laundry Services*.

The longer I stared at the rusty patches, the more they took on familiar shapes - a butterfly, a shoe, even a dog, just above where the back left wheel had been.

'What's inside?' I asked Toby, peering in. Something scuttered across the back of the van. I shuddered.

'It's just beetles,' Toby muttered. 'There seem to be quite a few of them, but they're harmless. Other than that, some tools and an old mattress.'

Milo was having a whale of a time kicking up leaves and sniffing the soil. When he noticed the van, he bounded straight in.

Despite the beetles and the old mattress, I was strangely taken with the van. It could easily be made homely with a blanket and some provisions, and I liked how it was tucked away, a true secret hideout. I wondered whether Toby had told anyone else about it.

Before I could ask, there was a sudden buzzing from his pocket. He fished out his phone.

'It's my mum. I have to head back. Are you coming?' he asked me.

'Yes.'

At the base of the riverbank, his wheelchair lodged itself in the mud, and I rushed to help, but once again, he'd already extracted himself before I got there.

As we drew closer to home, I was mesmerised by the glistening spinning of Toby's wheels and the squelching sound my shoes made as I trod on the patchwork of fallen leaves. Mud spattered my tights, my feet were soaked, and the tips of my big toes were numb from cold. Yet as we were walking, a warm sensation made me tingle – it was a feeling that I hadn't had for weeks.

And all my worries about Mum, about Lou, about the nightmare, about everything, faded for a couple of moments as Toby waved, before disappearing behind his front door.

Four

When we got indoors, the house was silent and empty, but I felt happy. Dad wasn't home yet, so I decided to make a start on my algebra homework. That way, when he got back, we could have dinner together and I could tell him about Toby and the swans.

I went upstairs to change out of my uniform. My room badly needed a clean. I could see dust gathered in the corners of my desk, and when I switched on the light, I could make out a brown stain where I'd spilled a cup of tea. The one part of my room that remained perfect, no matter how messy everything else was, was the wall above my bed.

If I told anybody that I usually enjoyed staring at this wall, they could be forgiven for thinking that I'd gone raving mad, but it's important to say that this isn't just your average bedroom wall. It's really the exact opposite - it's filled with colours and shapes and

textures, and it's my story. It's an unfinished story...
and it means so much to me for a lot of different reasons.

I was four when Mum started painting the mural,
and after that we'd always do it together. She would
stand by the wall in her baggy jumper, odd socks and
dungarees, holding an old kitchen plate on which she
mixed her colours. 'Let's paint some more of your story,
Izzy,' she'd say, smiling, and she'd tie up her long hair,
so that it didn't get in the way of her work. I always
thought she looked the most beautiful when she was
standing there, with the brush in her hand.

And even though I had itchy feet and could hardly
ever be still, I would sit for ages watching her paint. I
handed her the right sizes of brush and the colours that
she asked for - often I would guess them even before she
said them aloud. 'Colour me in!' I'd demand, as soon as
she'd finished sketching my outline. I couldn't stand
being kept grey and empty for longer than a few minutes.
She'd laugh at me and get started immediately. Often
she would colour in both versions of me - the picture
on the wall, and the real me, sitting cross-legged and
impatient on the bed. I would receive a sudden streak
of blue across my nose when I least expected it, and it
would make me chuckle.

Her painting grew and grew over the years. It was
divided into squares, each one an important event in

my life. My favourite was the square at the start - it showed Mum and Dad in hospital when I was born, Mum holding me on her lap, wrapped up cosy in a huge blanket, and Dad grinning. Apparently, I was the biggest baby on the ward, and the loudest.

That evening, as I collapsed on to the bed and looked up at it, I could tell immediately that something was *very wrong*. Yellow. I felt a spidery scuttling through my stomach as my eyes sought out the change. The yellow of my blanket had faded, as if all of the paint had drained from the plaster. The yellow had disappeared from the tulips in the hospital vase, and the small, dainty lampshade in the corner of the painted room... and that was just in the first square. I scanned the wall frantically. There was not a single place where yellow was still visible.

I turned up the light and checked it from all angles - it made no difference. A washed-out white had taken the place of the yellow, as if the entire image had been a stencil. I touched it, but there was nothing but smoothness beneath my fingertips. Could the paint have faded over the past few weeks and I just hadn't noticed? It was possible, of course, but was it likely? I decided to ask Dad to come and have a look as soon as he was home. It was always good to have a plan.

With the plan firmly in my mind, I went back

downstairs, poured out Milo's food and settled myself at the big dining room table with my books. It's strange how names stick to things. The last time the table had been used for dining would have been when there were still three of us eating at it. It would have been before the Blackest Day. Now, Dad and I ate at the table in the kitchen. I think we felt less lonely, in that cramped space. We could roll down the blinds and put something in the oven and the whole place enveloped us in a toasty glow.

I couldn't motivate myself to get started and I wondered what Toby was doing. My eyes kept darting to the kitchen window, to get a glimpse into the life of my new, mysterious neighbour.

And that was when it happened – I noticed Dad's shoes and the rucksack that he usually took to work.

I climbed the stairs slowly and knocked on his bedroom door.

'Dad, are you there? Can I come in?'

There was no noise from inside. I held my breath, but only for a moment, and then I opened the door. The room was dark and stuffy, and I groped for the light switch.

Dad was lying, still in his work clothes, on top of the duvet. There was a stack of papers next to him, some on the pillow; others had slipped on to the floor. I sat on the edge of the bed and took hold of his shoulders.

'Dad! Wake up! It's me!'

His eyelids fluttered and he shook his head.

'Dad?' Finally, his eyes opened fully and focused on me.

'Hi.' He smiled. 'You OK?' He sat up and looked at the black patch of window, confused.

'Yeah, I've just come back from school.'

'Ah. I must have... I must have fallen asleep. I came home a bit earlier today from the hospital and I lay down for a moment just to rest my eyes. What an idiot, eh? What's the time?'

I glanced at my watch.

'Time to eat?'

There was relief in Dad's eyes and shadows beneath them. He looked exhausted. I suddenly wanted to hug him, but he got there first, taking me into a bear-like embrace.

'I'll get dinner sorted,' he said. 'Then I'll have to stay up for a bit and work on this campaign. I promised Simon.'

I liked Simon, Dad's business partner. He was always cracking jokes. He and Dad had known each other since they went to school together, and decided to quit their jobs in big banks a year ago and start Project Elephant – an organisation which campaigns against animal poaching. When I first heard about

Dad's change of career, I only thought of poaching as a way of making eggs. Dad had explained that it meant the illegal hunting of animals, often those that were endangered.

Anyway, it was still just Simon and Dad on Project Elephant, and they'd been working horribly long hours at their office. It took Dad ages to travel each way, but since *that* day, he'd worked from home more and more.

I waited for him in the kitchen with a mug of tea and he came down a few minutes later, looking a bit more refreshed.

'How was your day, Diz?' he asked, ruffling my hair just a little too hard and beaming. He'd never stopped using the nickname that he'd given me when I was two, a whole decade ago. He called me that because I used to love to spin around in the garden until I was so dizzy that I collapsed on the ground and couldn't get back up.

'Dad, could you come and have a look...' I began, but when I looked again at the shadows under his eyes, the words stuck in my throat.

'Hmm?'

'It was all right,' I said instead.

For a moment, he sat there, nodding absent mindedly. Then his brow furrowed and he gave me a closer look.

'I went to see Mum today too,' I said. I felt as though I couldn't hold the information in any longer without telling him.

'How was it?' he asked quietly. 'Why did you go on your own?'

'I wasn't planning on going... it just sort of happened.'

'And they let you in?'

'Yes. I'm not sure the nurse knew that you weren't there. Maybe I'd just missed you before you left. I stepped into the room this time. I spoke to her.'

His eyes widened.

'And?'

He sounded hopeful, as if I was about to say something miraculous.

'And... nothing,' I said helplessly, and the anger boiled in my stomach. What did he expect? Did he think that I would walk in there and suddenly Mum would be better?

He opened and closed his mouth, as if he was planning to say something else, but decided against it.

'Let's put on some dinner,' he said. 'We must have something good in here that we can rustle up.'

Nanna Tessa, Dad's mum, had stayed with us in the weeks that followed the accident. She was an amazing cook and preparing food was what she loved. She made the most delicious dumplings from a recipe handed down from her own mum. Despite everything that had happened, she never failed to make a three-course dinner every single day she was with us. I could smell her delicious food from halfway down the road when I was walking home.

'Good food helps the soul,' she would tell us, serving up with a smile on her face. She liked to watch us eat what she'd made - all three of us: Milo, Dad and me. She said that was what made her most happy, but she was generally such a happy person.

It was only once that I saw Nanna's mask slip. I was in the garden and she was in the kitchen, stirring mushrooms, and she didn't know that anyone was watching her. I worried that something was wrong when I noticed her body shaking, and then I saw her wiping her eyes with her sleeve and I knew she was crying. I wanted to go in and hug her, but something stopped me. It was the same thing that had stopped me from going to hospital for a whole five weeks.

Before Nanna left to go back to Gramps, she'd frozen twelve portions of dumplings for us, which had lasted us all the way until last Tuesday. I opened the fridge, hopeful that we might have missed something else she'd left for us, but there were only eggs and a bag of old carrots that had started sprouting hairs.

'These look like they're ready to have babies,' Dad

said, picking one of them up with the tip of his thumb and forefinger. 'Gross or what? I really have to do the shopping. I'll go tomorrow.'

'We can have egg and chips.' I pulled the chips out of the freezer.

'Good thinking, Diz,' said Dad, taking out the frying pan and putting it on the hob. He tried to crack an egg on the side of it, but it slid out of his hand and landed on the floor.

'Don't worry, I'll do it.'

I emptied the chips into the dish and reached instinctively for the red elephant-shaped frying mould, which I knew would make Dad laugh. When it was ready, I dished everything up, grabbed the ketchup from the fridge and arranged it neatly on the tray along with glasses of water.

'Thanks,' said Dad. 'What would I do without you, eh? Starve, at the very least.'

After dinner, he settled on the sofa with his papers, and when I'd finished my homework, I switched on the TV, grateful that he hadn't gone back upstairs. I kept the volume down as much as possible so he could concentrate, but when I next glanced over, he'd tucked himself beneath the old throw that Milo loved to curl up on (even though he wasn't allowed on the sofa) and was fast asleep. I'd wanted to show Dad the mural, to see whether he could see the change too, but he had enough to think about already. It was something I'd have to figure out myself.

Five

There was smoke curling around the face of the shadow man. His threw his arms out towards me. He was tugging at me, trying to take me with him. I watched, frozen, as the muscles in his arms flexed and relaxed, flexed and relaxed. His sleeves were made of green cloth, and the fabric was coarse to touch. I pushed his arms away, but they came back for me even stronger.

'Don't look... don't look right!' he shouted.

The heat was rising... the unbearable, stifling heat... His face was so close now that I could hear him panting. Who was he? I wanted to see his features, though I was terrified of them too. He blurred before me, blurred and shifted until he was no longer there at all.

I'd held my eyes shut long after the alarm went off, trying to shake off the nightmare for the second night in a row, and praying that the mural would have gone back to normal overnight. But the spiders scrambled into life as soon as I dared to look up at my favourite wall.

Not only was the yellow gone, the green of the grass in the next picture had also dissolved. This one was of me, aged six, sitting in the garden and giving myself a haircut. I'd insisted on playing Peter Pan in the reception play and I was convinced that I needed to be as realistic as possible – devoted to theatre from an early age. Except it now looked as if I was sitting on a plane of snow. The spiders stomped, moving from my stomach to my chest, leaving a horrible tickling ache.

And then, suddenly, it hit me – the shadow man from the nightmare must have something to do with the disappearance of the colours. He had appeared just as they had started to disappear. It couldn't be a coincidence. And if *only I* had experienced the nightmare, maybe *only I* knew the colours were gone. Of course I could ask Dad to have a look to see if he noticed, but somehow I already knew what he'd say. No one else would understand about the colour thief. But who was he and why was he stealing from me? My head spun with unanswered questions.

When I made my way downstairs, I found the kitchen empty and the sink still filled with dirty dishes from last night. Dad's chipped mug rested on the sideboard, perilously close to the edge. Mum had bought it for him. The picture of Batman and Robin had almost entirely rubbed off, but the speech bubble with the words, 'You're my sidekick for life', was just about legible. I emptied the dregs of coffee and put it into the dishwasher. I hadn't seen the mug in weeks. Even more than the dining table, it belonged in the past. What had made him take it out of the cupboard now?

I skipped breakfast, ushered Milo indoors and got myself ready quicker than ever before. Toby was waiting for me. Lou was not. I think I'd already known she wouldn't turn up.

Toby must have been watching for me to leave the house, because he came out of his front door at the very same moment that I left mine.

'Meet me by the van after school?' he asked. 'I've got a plan of action to feed Spike.'

'Of course. I'll be there.'

'Great.' He smiled, the same mysterious smile as the previous day, and I set off, feeling much happier. I made it to school a few minutes before the bell.

'All hail,' said Frank, as I walked in. He was fiddling with something on his nose and when he pulled his hands away I thought that his face was covered with blobs of toothpaste. It was only when I got closer that I noticed they were stick-on boils. He looked so ridiculous that I burst out laughing. Maybe sitting next to him wouldn't be so bad, after all. I couldn't remember the last time Lou had made me laugh.

'Double, double toil and trouble; Fire burn, and cauldron bubble.'

'Eh?'

'I'm going for the role of one of the three witches,' he said. 'Who said that they have to be witches? They could be wizards. In Shakespeare's time all the roles were played by men anyway.'

'That's true.' I was impressed he knew. It wasn't something we'd covered in English. Who would have thought - Frank the Skank, a Shakespeare fan? 'But what do you mean, you're "going for the role"?'

'The auditions - they're tomorrow, aren't they? I'm preparing early.'

Macbeth. How could I have forgotten about the auditions?

As if guessing my thoughts, Lou came to hover by my desk. I noticed that she'd curled her lashes today. No wonder she hadn't had time to pick me up on the way to school.

'I suppose you're auditioning for Lady Macbeth, are you?' she asked, raising an eyebrow.

'Yeah, I...' I didn't feel like admitting that I'd forgotten about it and was completely unprepared.

'Just to let you know that Jemima is going for it too. She's semi-professional, so, you know... you might want to choose a different role, to give yourself more of a chance of getting it. Maybe Lady Macduff or one of the chambermaids?'

'What do you mean "semi-professional"?'

'She's been going to Saturday drama school since the age of five, Izzy. There's really no point in you trying.'

I looked into Lou's eyes to check whether she really meant what she said. I still half-expected her to start laughing and tell me that it had all been a joke and that of course she was my friend.

'I'd like to give it a go, anyway. I've always wanted to play Lady Macbeth and it would be stupid not to even try.'

'Even though you know you don't stand a chance?' Lou interrupted. She clicked her tongue impatiently.

'It may only be small, but I do have a chance.'

'Whatever.' She shrugged her shoulders. She was about to walk away when something made me grab her.

'Why are you being like this?' I whispered. 'I'm just the same as I used to be.'

She looked at me pityingly, but I refused to give up. 'Couldn't we just start over? Why don't you come round to mine on Friday night? We can walk Milo and watch horror films. Dad won't mind.'

'No thanks, Izzy,' she said. 'You honestly think that walking your dog would be the way that I'd like to spend a Friday night? You're weirder than I thought. Anyway, I have other plans.'

'What other plans?' I was surprised to hear myself sounding so needy. Heads began to turn as we suddenly became the centre of attention. Lou's face was flushed.

'If you must know, I'm staying at Jemima's,' she hissed. 'It's her brother's birthday and we're planning to sneak into the party. There's going to be a proper DJ and everything. If you're so desperate for somebody to spend time with, maybe you could invite Frank to yours for a bit of a horror-movie sesh? He looks just the sort to be into some crazy vampire films, and if you play your cards right, who knows what might happen?' she said, winking at me sarcastically.

She said it so loudly that most people in the class heard.

A red rage erupted inside me and climbed slowly up my throat, the lava making me feel as if I was going to be sick. I pushed past Lou and ran blindly out of the classroom, stopping only when I got far down the empty corridor, my hands on my knees. I heard nothing but my breath – my fast, angry breath.

Why did she say that? Why did she have to say that

in front of the whole class? We had been so close that we had practically lived in each other's houses. We'd shared everything from clothes to the contents of our pencil cases. Back in primary school we even had our own secret language – nobody else had ever deciphered it. Mum and Dad had always been nice to her. And Shelley had taken me everywhere with Lou – shopping, cinema, concerts... How was it so easy for Lou just to forget all that?

My back slid down the wall until I was sitting on the dusty floor. Slowly, my breathing returned to normal and when I looked up, I saw that I'd gone further than I thought. I was in the history corridor with its display on 'Milton School Through the Years'. Mr McKenzie always went on about how we were walking through history. 'Milton Secondary School may not have been around in the time of Milton the poet,' he would say, 'but it's almost a hundred and fifty years old.'

Now, as I looked at the display, I saw the old merging with the new. The black and white photos of lacrosse players from the 1920s didn't look all that different to the recent pictures of the Year Nine trip to Egypt, in which the once-yellow pyramids were grey and faded. Like my mural, all their colour had seeped away.

'Hey! There you are.'

I spun round to see Frank running towards me.

I wondered if he'd been sent to get me. I waited for the snide remark, but it didn't come.

'Are you all right?' he asked. 'You're not going to let her get to you, are you?'

I was so shocked, I didn't know how to answer.

A blush spread over Frank's neck and face.

'I saw you last year in *A Midsummer Night's Dream*,' he continued. 'You were really good. Scrap that - you were *awesome*. Don't let her put you off. She's an idiot.'

For a moment, I couldn't speak. But then my anger dissolved, and I felt almost normal. I'd clearly been wrong about Frank. Lou had made him out to be nothing but a disgusting skank, but there were already things that proved her wrong. He was into Shakespeare, he'd seen me in a play, he'd come after me when he saw I was upset. And really there was nothing particularly skanky about him - in fact, his dark mop of hair sort of suited him.

Frank put out his hand to help me to my feet. I hesitated only for a second. Then I grabbed it and, together, we walked back to class.

A group of Year Elevens trudged past on their way to the hockey field. I recognised the tall one as the Deputy Head Boy, Cormack Griffiths. Most of the girls from Year Nine upwards were madly in love with him. Personally, I didn't see the attraction - he was the size of a netball post, and had a permanently mocking expression. He looked as if he was always about to say something horrible.

He whistled as he walked past us, and told his friend, 'Young love.'

I usually would have turned crimson, but this time his words didn't get to me.

'Thanks,' I muttered to Frank when they'd gone. 'Thanks for coming after me.'

'It's nothing. You would have done the same.'

Yesterday that probably wouldn't have been true, but so many things had changed in a day.

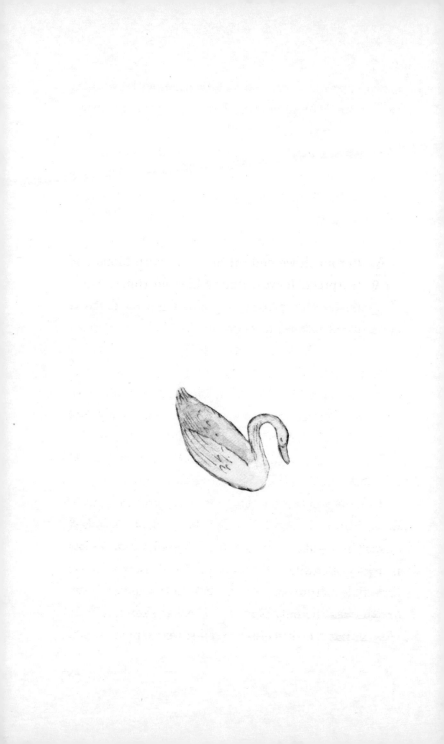

Six

After lunch we had art and I sat with Mona and Harpreet. It was almost like old times. Mona showed me a photo of the new puppy that her parents had got over the weekend. She was exactly the same breed as Milo, but tiny. So cute.

Then, when I'd been expecting the arrival of the supply teacher, Mr Leah came in. He'd been off since the start of term, because his wife had had a baby, and I hadn't known he'd be back so soon.

He grinned and told us about baby Lucy and asked us all how we'd been getting on without him.

Several people around the class shouted that they'd missed him, though I doubted that any of them had missed him quite as much as me. Mr Leah was *awesome* in every meaning of the word. He drew the most incredible pictures of various parts of the human body, and he was the only person who could sketch a hand so well that it looked almost as if it were a photograph.

But not only was he amazing at drawing, he made every lesson seem as if it was an adventure.

We'd just finished doing self-portraits, and without his encouragement, we somehow couldn't concentrate and we'd spent all of our time in the past few art lessons doodling and messing around.

I was glad when Mr Leah told us that he'd missed us too.

'Right, let's finish mounting the self-portraits you've worked on and next week I'm going to get you started on something new. What do you say?'

'Sounds good,' said someone at the front. 'What will it be?'

'Ah, I was going to keep it a surprise, but I'll give you a clue and you can go away and see whether you get it. Let's see... it will be working in the style of a particular artist. And this artist was preoccupied with dreams and is known for painting some very unusual clocks. Don't think about it now. Jot it down in your homework diary and see if you can solve it over the weekend.'

I thought about Mr Leah's mystery as I walked home from school. Dreams and clocks were linked to the colour thief. He'd appeared first in a dream, which was really more of a nightmare, and when he'd faded from my mind, the first things I always saw were the luminous numerals on my clock. The spiders wrestled in my stomach at the thought of him.

But they were defeated when I opened the door to let Milo out. He brushed up against me fondly and then dutifully followed me to the river, getting more and more excited. He bounced along the path between the houses. He was running so fast that he slipped and ended up rolling down into the shrubbery where we'd first seen Spike.

I bolted after him, scared he might have fallen into the water, but by the time I arrived, he was already shaking himself off and trotting in the direction of the bridge.

Toby was waiting by the van as we'd agreed, holding something long and pointed in his hand. As I drew closer I could see that it was a fishing rod.

'Hi,' he said. 'You came.'

'Of course. Why do we need that?'

'It's for Spike. He always loses the fight over food with his brothers and sisters, so this will be a good way of getting it to him directly. I just have to figure out the mechanism. It belonged to my uncle. I've never used it before.'

He pulled on a latch, there was a clicking sound and suddenly the wire began to wind itself round the spool. He nodded, satisfied.

'I've been doing a bit of research on swans,' he told me. 'I thought the more we knew, the more we'd be able to help him.'

'Great. What did you find out?'

'Loads. Do you know how old swans are when their feathers turn white?'

'Ummm... about a year?' I actually had no idea.

'That's what I thought too, but it's earlier - six months. That's when their parents know that they're ready to go out into the world alone. The undersides of their feathers turn white first. And guess what they like to eat?'

'Bread?'

'Weirdly, no. They eat lettuce, spinach (yuck) and potato.'

'Gross. At least we'll know what to bring him.'

'Exactly. Right, I think we're ready. Let's go down to the water and try out the rod. Do you mind holding it? It's a bit difficult to carry it and push my wheels at the same time.'

'Sure.'

'I could have got an electric one,' he told me through deep breaths, 'but I like the challenge, you know. My arms could do with the exercise too. The worst is when it rains, because then I get covered with mud and splashback from the ground.'

I nodded, unsure of what to say. The truth was that I had no idea what it must be like for him.

I followed Toby towards Spike's mulberry bush. The water was choppier today, some serious-looking ripples on its surface. Mr Joshi, the shopkeeper at the bottom of the street, told me that once a grown man was swept away on the current and dragged more than ten kilometres downstream before he was rescued. Judging by the speed of the water this afternoon, it definitely would have been possible.

The mother swan was in a pocket of still water among the reeds, sleeping with her head tucked under her wing. Three of her babies were snoozing on either side of her and another was in the long river grass. Spike was nowhere in sight.

'Where are you?' I asked aloud. I trod through the undergrowth on the riverbank, pulling the grass apart. Nothing. Panic rose in my chest. Had he fallen prey to the treacherous current?

'Look, there's another swan,' whispered Toby. 'It could be the dad. You can see that his neck is thicker, and he has a bigger black bit at the base of the bill.'

I looked in the direction Toby was pointing, as the mother swan went to join the other swan. They were beautiful, but even they seemed slower today, stalled by the rippling water. I could make out a couple of bobbing grey heads near them, but no sign of Spike. Why weren't they doing anything to find him?

Suddenly, there was a splash and before I knew what was happening, Milo was in the water swimming to the centre of the river. I froze.

'Milo! Come back here...'

Already the current was carrying him away. He struggled against it, but it was no use.

'Milo!' I screamed. 'Milo!'

There was a scramble on the riverbank followed by a second splash. I thought it might have been the mother swan but then, with horror, I saw the empty wheelchair with Toby's glasses and hoodie lying on the seat, I turned back to the river and watched helplessly as he made his way swiftly towards Milo. I could see the strong movement of his arms and his muscular back as he pulled himself through the water. He seemed to reach Milo in less than ten strokes and held firmly on to him as he began to swim to shore again.

I unclenched my fists and allowed my muscles to relax. Then they disappeared behind a clump of bushes and the river became silent.

There was nothing but the wind in the trees and the hum of traffic in the distance.

'Toby!' *Please be all right. Please be all right. Please be all right.* I had two choices. I could run and get help, or

I could try and get in myself to rescue them.

I wasn't a good swimmer so I decided on the first option. I was already running up the path towards the road, when I heard a shout. I turned to see Toby pulling himself out of the water. Milo stood, dazed and shivering, on the riverbank.

'Thank goodness!' I ran to help him. Part of me wanted to shout at him for being so stupid, but he'd been brave too – he'd rescued Milo and it seemed that they were both all right.

'It was OK,' said Toby, panting. 'But for a small dog like him it would have been pretty scary.'

His hair was stuck to his forehead in sodden strands and his eyes looked bewildered without the protection of his glasses.

'Thank you,' I said. It was such a meaningless couple of words for what he'd just done. 'I can't believe you did that.'

'It's fine. I could see he was in trouble.'

Toby propped his glasses back on his nose and they promptly steamed up. Water was pouring from his trousers and I instinctively lifted his feet and wrung out first one trouser leg, then the other. His knees felt sharp and thin through the fabric. He was shivering badly, so I took off my coat and draped it round his shoulders. The awful possibility of what might have happened was replaying itself on a loop through my mind and I had to force myself to breathe slowly – in through my nose, out through my mouth.

It was OK. Nothing bad happened. It wouldn't be like...

Toby's teeth chattered, but he had a grin on his face and a faraway look as if he was thinking about something.

'Are you all right?' I asked. 'We need to get back home. It's freezing!'

But I could tell that he wasn't listening.

'It reminded me a bit of the old days. You know... before.'

'Before?'

'Pass me my hoodie. I want to show you something,' he said, furiously rubbing the goose bumps on his arms. There were wet leaves still stuck to his back, which left muddy stamps when I peeled them off. Mum and I used to make leaf stencils when I was little. We would walk together collecting a bunch of skeleton leaves and press them hard on to a piece of paper to make patterns.

I took the green hoodie from his wheelchair and Toby dug his wet hand into one of the pockets and pulled out a crumpled photo of a boy in a football strip running after a ball. It took me a moment to recognise him.

'I was team captain. I used to win awards in swimming too. At least that's something that I can still do.'

I stared at the photo. I felt so sad for him that I didn't know how to respond.

In the end, I pulled my eyes away from the determined sports star in the picture, and handed him back to Toby.

'You're brilliant,' I said quietly, 'but you're also about to freeze and so is Milo. We need to get home.'

The discarded fishing rod lay propped up against the mulberry bush. I gazed at the darkening water. There was still no sign of Spike. But I was surprised to find that I no longer felt as frightened for him as I had done when we'd first arrived. Something made me believe that Spike was stronger than we thought. I looked at Toby and knew he was thinking the same.

'We'll just have to try again,' he insisted. 'We'll leave our stuff in the van and come tomorrow or the day after. But first I need to get myself back in the driving seat. Will you help me, please? I'm much better at getting off this thing than I am getting on. I need someone to hold it steady for me.'

'Sure.'

I wedged my foot behind the back wheels of his chair, keeping one eye on Milo, who was busy licking himself after his ordeal. Toby heaved himself up and I had barely managed to step back, when he was already on his way up to the paved path.

To my amazement, he beckoned to Milo and, within

moments, my dog was sitting on his lap, his head curled against his saviour's chest. I suppose that I normally would have felt jealous, but things were different because it was Toby.

'Won't your mum be mad about you being all wet?' I asked him, when we were almost at the main road. My footprints left a speckled pattern on either side of Toby's wheel tracks.

'Nah. She's not the type to get mad. She usually just worries loads, but that's about things that haven't happened yet. She won't worry if she sees I'm safe.'

She sounded so much like my mum. I hoped I'd get to meet her someday soon.

'You know you're always welcome to come to ours,' Toby said, again guessing what I'd been thinking. 'Mum's been going on about wanting to meet some of the new neighbours. I think she's feeling a bit lonely. She doesn't know anyone around here.'

'Do *you* feel lonely?' I asked him.

He turned to me. 'I did for a bit. I don't so much any more.'

He did a funny gentlemanly flourish with his hand, which implied that I should follow him in through his front door, but I checked my watch and saw that it was getting late. Dad would probably be home from the hospital and wondering what I was doing.

'I can't tonight,' I told him, grabbing Milo's lead. 'I'll definitely see you tomorrow, though.'

I turned to make my way home, still thinking about Dad, and slowly, the spidery sensation started up in my stomach once more. I knew that he would want to talk about Mum and the hospital. I breathed in and braced myself.

Seven

When I opened the back door, I immediately sensed that something had changed. The house smelled different. There was a scent of flowers and something sharp and tangy that I vaguely recognised.

I walked into the kitchen to find Aunty Lyn in full tidying-up mode, spraying detergent on every surface.

'Izzy, there you are, love! I was beginning to worry. Where have you been?'

She embraced me so hard that I felt winded.

Aunty Lyn was Dad's sister, but she couldn't have been more different to him. Where Dad was easy-going, she was ruthlessly organised.

When I was smaller, I used to think of her as one of those old-fashioned watchmakers - the ones who are always fiddling with the screws in the backs of clocks, making sure that every tick-tock is as even as can be.

Except Aunty Lyn looked nothing like a watchmaker. In fact, she didn't even look like an aunt should look. She wore matching slim-fitted trouser suits and heels, and her hair was perfectly arranged in short ginger layers falling like waves around her face, not a single strand out of place. She always had her dark red lipstick on, even to do the vacuuming.

'What are you doing here?' I asked her.

'That's a lovely welcome, isn't it?'

'Sorry. Sorry.'

'I've come to stay with you and your dad for a while,' she said brightly, though her smile was forced.

And then she looked at me, and enveloped me in an unexpected hug. It was so sudden that I didn't have a chance to dodge.

'How have you been, Izzy? Honestly?' she asked, looking deep into my eyes.

I stayed quiet. What was there left to say?

'I know you didn't want to speak to me on the phone, and that's OK. But I want you to know that I'm here for you, any time that you need me.'

'Thank you,' I said. 'How long are you staying?'

It sounded unwelcoming, and I knew it, but Aunty Lyn didn't flinch.

'It's not for ever, it's just to, you know, help out a bit.'

'To... help out?'

'Yes,' she said. 'Don't worry. I'm not going to interfere with things – I'm just going to support you with some of the day-to-day stuff.'

Of course she would interfere – interfering was what Aunty Lyn did best. I felt tired just thinking about how regimented life would become under her reign, but it looked like I had no other option. A part of me had to admit that maybe it would be good to have somebody making decisions for a bit. I felt like they'd been taking up a huge amount of space in my head and I needed that space to think about the colour thief.

'Goodness, your uniform. You're going to have to take that off, Izzy. Here, go upstairs and get changed. I'm putting on a wash, so I'll pop that in with it. And put that dog out in the garden. He looks filthy. I don't want him muddying the kitchen floor. I've just washed it.'

'But he needs to get warm and dry, and he always has his dinner in the kitchen.' The regime was beginning already.

'OK – put it in his bowl then and give it to him outside. I'll dry his paws afterwards and he can come back in for the evening.'

'Where's Dad?'

'He's at the hospital, darling. He may be there a while.'

I'm not sure why I even asked. Dad had been at

the hospital every day for the past forty. Yesterday in maths, I worked out that Mum had been there almost six weeks, or nearly a thousand hours. Dad used to ask me every morning to go with him and every morning I pretended not to hear. After a while he stopped asking.

The truth was, I couldn't. I couldn't bear seeing her so pale and fragile and still. And not going to see her now, after having been once, was worse than before when I hadn't been at all. It had been my fault and I couldn't explain that to Dad so I avoided the subject altogether. If he was mad at me for not going, he didn't say anything.

'I'm going to pop out in a second to do the shopping. You hardly had anything in the fridge,' said Aunty Lyn.

'I got milk and bread the other day and there's the veg from last week...' I began. I stopped when I heard how feeble it sounded, and remembered the hairy carrots. She was right.

'Honestly, I don't know how you've been managing. I mean, if I lived here...'

But you don't live here, I thought. *And you don't know what it's been like. We've been managing, Dad and me.* I wished someone would recognise that.

I left Aunty Lyn to write her shopping list, dried Milo with an old towel and let him out into the garden.

'I'm sorry,' I whispered into the soft fur of his ears.

I picked him up and pulled him on to the bench swing in the garden, because he loved to sit on it. It was one of my own favourite spots. I could lie across it and be swayed gently from side to side, and look up at the perfect, undisturbed stretch of sky above. I could get lost in the endless summer blue, or watch pictures formed by the clouds in the autumn. Once I even managed to get a photo on Mum's phone of a cloud that looked exactly like Milo mid-jump. On a clear night I could make out all the main stars - the Big Dipper, Orion and Cancer.

Today, the sky was grey, but I shuffled into position. There was the dark shadow on the left armrest, which I knew had been made by our heads. Mum's and mine. We would snuggle up, Mum on the left side, me on the right and she would sketch in her pad. Sometimes it was an abstract thing from a dream and other times it was what she could see, like the sunflowers that bloomed at the end of the garden in late August, or the neighbours' cat sleeping in the middle of the lawn. Sometimes she would sketch me. I would read or listen to stuff on my headphones and watch her as she worked. I never felt calmer or happier.

That dark shadow made me miss her so powerfully that I got up suddenly and went into the kitchen.

'I want to go and see her,' I announced to Aunty Lyn. 'Could you drive me to the hospital, please?'

She stopped midway through her shopping list.

'Or I could just walk there.'

'No. I'll drive you on the way to the shops.' She didn't sigh or tut. She just got her coat and car keys and we left.

I saw Dad through the glass. He sat on the edge of the bed, holding Mum's good hand in between his. He was talking, although I couldn't hear the words. I saw him stroke her cheek, the same way he used to when he came home and was leaning in for a kiss. She would sometimes pull away. 'Stop tickling me with your beard!' she'd say, laughing.

I half-expected her to do that now, but she just lay still, so still. Then Dad saw me and smiled, beckoning me to join him.

'I'm glad you're here,' he said. 'Speak to your mum. Speak to her. The doctors say that she might be able to hear it in her subconscious. Sometimes little things like that can help people who are... in this state.'

I swallowed hard. My throat was dry. I opened my mouth but I had nothing to say. I felt as though I was being asked to act in front of an audience, though no script had been given to me.

'I'll wait outside,' Dad said, as the silent seconds stretched between us. 'I know you probably want to be alone with her.'

I was left in the room with Mum for the second time in two days. The heart monitor beeped mercilessly. It was good that it beeped, I repeated over and over in my head. It was a good thing.

There was so much I wanted to tell her. She would have been the first to know about Toby, and I felt bad for having told Dad and Aunty Lyn before her. And I was scared about the audition – I didn't realise until now quite how scared. I felt that when I got on stage, I would end up being bland and boring... and grey – like the outline of a person that Mum had drawn before she started painting, or like the images the colour thief left behind. There was nothing worse in acting than being boring.

'I'm scared, Mum,' I whispered.

I held her hand. It was warmer than I had expected, and it encouraged me to keep talking. 'I don't know what to do about *Macbeth*. Lou doesn't want me to do it, though she knows that I've been looking forward to it for months, even if I did forget about the auditions. And even if she hadn't said that, I'm not sure whether I'd be any good any more. It's a big role and I'm sure there are loads of people who'd be better than me.'

I wanted more than anything for her to say, 'Diz, you're being ridiculous, aren't you? You'll be amazing, and you know it, no matter what anyone says.' And then I wanted her to ruffle my hair and say that I should recite the hardest speech in front of her.

So I imagined that she *had* said that. I stood up and shut my eyes. 'OK, Mum.' I began: 'Out, out damned spot...' I'd barely managed those four words when my eyes flew open and I saw the reality: her lying there with her eyes shut and her face expressionless. What had I done? And then the red anger started bubbling inside me, because of course there was no reaction from her at all. I thought that I might at least get a feeling - that her advice might seep into me, that I would understand what to do. But I was filled with nothing except the awful redness which crashed down on me with an almighty force. The high-pitched beeps grew louder and louder in my head. I picked up my coat and quickly walked out.

Eight

I went to my room the moment we got back home. I lay on my bed trying to get the image of the hospital with Mum in it out of my head. I thought about Toby and the swans and, slowly, slowly, felt calmer - we would find Spike and help him. I was somehow certain that we would. Milo padded into my room and settled at the foot of the bed, by my feet.

I went over to the big bookcase and pulled out Mum's battered copy of *Macbeth*, remembering that I'd marked Lady Macbeth's sleepwalking scene with one of Dad's Project Elephant brochures. Instead of focusing on memorising the lines for the audition, I picked up the brochure and began flicking through.

"'Ivory has been prized for thousands of years in certain cultures, and elephants have been killed for it,'" I read. "'Around twenty thousand elephants were killed last year for their tusks.'"

I looked at the number in horror. Surely it couldn't

be true? But Dad never lied – I trusted him. I couldn't imagine anyone wanting to kill these beautiful animals. I looked at the photograph of a mother elephant with her baby. She had a smattering of deep wrinkles around her eyes and she looked as if she was laughing. I opened my desk drawer and pulled out my red folder. I flicked through it frantically, worrying that I had accidentally binned it, but there it was. The elephant card Mum had made me for my tenth birthday. I'd had an obsession with elephants then, after one had eaten from my hand in the safari park. Dad had told me about how endangered they were, and looked at Mum meaningfully. It turned out that he'd already spoken to Simon about starting Project Elephant. But in the meantime, I had the card she had painted for me, each wrinkle carefully drawn on to the skin, in thick pencil.

I stared at the elephant for a long while and then tucked the card carefully back into the red folder.

She was everywhere and yet so unreachable.

I found that I couldn't speak about her when I sat down at the dinner table half an hour later, even though I could sense that Dad wanted to. Instead, I talked about Toby.

'He's moved into Mason's old place?' asked Aunty Lyn. She'd insisted on sitting at Nanna Tessa's table in the dining room. 'About time, eh? That's been empty for ages. They'll have loads of work to do on the house, though. It's an absolute ruin.'

'Is he a good lad, this Toby?' asked Dad.

'Yes and yes,' I said, putting a mouthful of Aunty Lyn's spaghetti bolognese into my mouth. I hadn't eaten anything so good since Nanna left, and I finished my helping before Dad and Aunty Lyn had even managed to work their way through half of theirs.

'That's great,' said Dad.

'And how are you managing with everything at school, Izzy?' asked Aunty Lyn, her eyebrows meeting in the centre of her forehead in an expression of concern. It was an innocent question, but I could sense the pity in her voice.

'I'm managing OK,' I snapped. Couldn't they just spend a few minutes talking about other things? Didn't they see that was what I wanted?

'Are you on top of your homework, darling? Is there anything that you want me to help with?'

'No, I'm good. I'll do it in a sec.'

'Great,' said Aunty Lyn. 'What lessons did you have today?'

I just wanted to go upstairs, but they still hadn't finished eating and I didn't want to be completely rude.

'Umm... English, history, art...'

'Art?' asked Dad. 'What are you doing in art?'

'We're starting a new project – Mr Leah hasn't told us what it is yet. We're supposed to guess and he's given us two clues. Apparently, we'll be working on something linked to an artist who focused on dreams and drew clocks.'

'Dalí,' said Dad.

'Dalí?'

'Salvador Dalí. *The Persistence of Memory*.' His eyes lit up.

'Really? What's *The Persistence of Memory*?'

'It's the name of a painting. I'm sure you've seen it before. It's very typical of Dalí because it contains several floppy clocks – I was always taken by those clocks. They're so strange and yet so accurate.'

'What do you mean? Why are they accurate?'

'Because they show how time is relative. Here, have a look.' He took out his phone and brought the painting up on the screen to show me. He was right – I'd seen it before, although I wasn't sure where.

Aunty Lyn peered over my shoulder as she collected the plates, fussing with a dishcloth over the rings made by our water tumblers.

'I wonder why it's called that,' she said.

'To me, it's simple,' Dad replied, looking at the picture. 'It's because sometimes your memories are constantly with you, whether you want them to be or not. Time passes, the clocks move on, but you remain stuck there – your useless, floppy clock always telling the same time. And even if you think you've finally escaped, your memories always catch up with you. They come in bursts when you least expect it.'

Dad came with me to my room after dinner and he brought Milo with him, against Aunty Lyn's orders.

'You OK, Diz?' he asked, as he sat on the edge of the bed, Milo in his lap.

'Sort of,' I said. 'You?'

He smiled sadly and turned his gaze in the direction of the mural. I waited for him to say something, but his expression didn't change. It was obvious he couldn't see that the colours had disappeared. I felt lonelier than ever.

'Been better.'

I squeezed his hand and rested my head against his shoulder.

'I've always liked that one best,' he said, pointing to the picture of me as Juliet with long, flowing hair, standing on the balcony, looking down. It was my favourite role out of all of the ones I'd played.

'That wig was so tickly. I felt like I still had the itch for days afterwards.'

'I remember. You were scratching yourself so much

we thought you might have nits. Mum got you that special shampoo, didn't she?'

'Yeah, and Milo spilled it and it smelled horrendous.'

'Hey, you haven't given up on the acting, have you?' he asked. 'You know it's not just me who thinks you're absolutely specsational at it.'

I smiled. The word had slipped out when Dad had seen me in my first play, many years ago. He wasn't sure whether he wanted to say spectacular or sensational, so he'd blended them and it had stuck.

'You know I'm still your biggest fan. Look at all of these performances. When I was your age, I'd barely been in a Christmas play, and that was as King Herod's servant. I didn't even speak - just held his cloak for him. You have real talent, you know - don't waste it.'

He wasn't my biggest fan, of course. I knew that role belonged to Mum, but it made me feel better. I thought about what he'd said long after he'd left the room.

Lou's words came echoing back too, but this time they had no impact. I didn't care that Jemima was 'semi-professional'. I was going to go for Lady Macbeth.

Nine

I breathed in the awful, stifling heat. It filled my insides, expanded in my chest and with it began the spidery sprawl of panic. My watery eyes struggled to make out the edges of things – there were only yellows and oranges now, clouded with grey. My hands groped helplessly through the colours like blind explorers.

'Don't look right!'

But I wouldn't listen to him. I looked right and I wished that I hadn't.

Because to the right there was nothing but red; nothing but red and an aching emptiness.

'Don't look...!' shouted the colour thief. But he was too late.

3.57 a.m.

'You ready?' asked Frank, the moment I arrived in class.

I shook my head. I'd tried to go through the speech again this morning, but I'd been too preoccupied with the mural. The blissful minutes after waking had been filled with forgetfulness, then, as I'd opened my eyes, I was jolted back to reality. Blue. The royal blue of my Juliet dress had gone, as had the blue of the sky in the hair-cutting picture, and the blue of the tiny bag which had held my first few baby teeth, with its carefully drawn navy string. The blue had joined yellow and green. A terrible blankness enveloped my wall.

My legs were weak as I climbed out of bed, but I tried to force the colour thief out of my mind. Lady Macbeth had to come first.

'I've given up on being a witch,' Frank continued, not noticing my panic. 'It's too much effort... Maybe I can get out of the whole thing and pretend to be ill. I'm particularly good at acting someone with a bout of food poisoning. Hey, maybe I could be that Banquo guy? You know, the one Macbeth kills?'

He began clutching his stomach and making retching noises. Within a moment, he had fallen dramatically to the floor and was writhing around bumping into desks. I paid no attention. Was I deluding myself that I was actually in with a chance? There were so many reasons to abandon the attempt.

'Hey,' said Frank on the way over to the hall. His cheeks were flushed as he handed me a folded piece of paper. I unravelled it to find a picture of a figure in a long, swirly cloak standing on stage with loads of people around her, their mouths open in big 'O's.

'Why are they scared?' I whispered to him.

'They're not - they're in awe of how awesome you are.'

He didn't have a chance to say anything more, because Mr Winch announced, 'Right, the day of judgement - auditions.' There were a couple of excited yelps, but they were drowned by a much larger number of groans.

'OK, hands up who's not interested in any of the named parts and wants to be involved in the lighting, costume or set design?' I was on the verge of putting my hand up, but at the last minute, I stopped myself. Mr Winch ushered those who didn't want to audition to one side of the hall, split them into groups and got them working on different projects to do with the play. Not satisfied with his writhing bout, Frank had acquired a packet of fake blood from somewhere and was busily biting into it.

Those who remained were separated into the roles they wanted to try for. Jemima gave me a meaningful look, a half-smile playing across her lips.

Now that I noticed them sitting together, speaking in hushed whispers, I could see the similarities between her and Lou. They'd practically merged into each other with their high-heeled polished shoes, sheets of poker-straight hair and mocking expressions. They even had the same phone covers in a leopard print pattern.

Maybe I should have noticed much earlier that Lou was swapping Jemima into her best friend slot. The signs had been there, I hadn't been paying attention.

Mr Winch was back. 'I'd like you to read the "Out, damned spot!" speech, which is when Lady Macbeth has lost her mind and is haunted by the visions of all the people she's persuaded her husband to kill. You can take a few moments to prepare and then I'd like you to perform it to the rest of the class.'

I'd memorised the whole speech, but my mind was as empty as the spaces left by the vanishing greens, blues and yellows on my wall. There was no way I'd be able to do it.

Then Frank shuffled along and sat next to me, giving my hand a tiny squeeze, and I saw Mona showing me her crossed fingers behind her back. And all of a sudden, the lines I thought I'd forgotten rearranged themselves into the right order in my head.

Nora, a tall, thin girl who'd just joined our class at the beginning of term went first of the three candidates for Lady Macbeth. I could tell that she immediately regretted going for the role. Her hands shook as she held the script, and she frequently stuttered, having to repeat lines several times. When she'd finished, she sat back down in the audience and hid her head in her hands. My stomach tightened as I imagined myself exactly like her in a few minutes' time.

Jemima was next. She read boldly and moved confidently around the stage, her eyes wandering like those of a mad woman. The way she relentlessly washed her hands sent a shudder down my spine. There was no doubt that she had been well-trained. Mr Winch nodded approvingly, narrowed his eyes and scribbled notes as he watched. She was a tough act to follow.

This was it. As I walked on to the stage, I closed my eyes. Blood thudded in my ears and then a thought wormed its way into my mind. We weren't that different, really, Lady Macbeth and I. We had both done something terrible, something truly bad. And what was more, we were being punished for it. Lady Macbeth with her spot, and me with Mum. Before I knew it, I was speaking – and whether it was my own voice, or Lady Macbeth's, I wasn't sure. The feelings of guilt poured from my mouth, the audience disappeared from before my eyes and the background noise became silence. And as I spoke a memory came to the surface of my mind...

a memory from before. It was the final curtain call from last year's play, and Mum was sitting in the front row, clapping like crazy.

I held on to this memory throughout my speech, focussing on the pride on Mum's face. I could reach her. I could. Before I knew it, it was all over.

There was a second's pause before my class erupted into the loudest applause that I had ever heard. Harpreet was whistling with admiration and Mona gave me the double thumbs-up.

'Unreal!' shouted Frank. Some of the girls in the back row gave me a standing ovation and Mr Winch looked as if he was about to explode.

'Magnificent, Izzy! Absolutely magnificent.'

I could barely keep up with what was happening. I went quietly to my seat and people in the rows behind patted me on the back. I could hear a couple of girls commenting on how frightening I'd been.

'Quieten down, everyone!' Mr Winch ordered, but the tail end of Lou's sentence, as she spoke to Jemima, could be heard in the silence that followed... 'Let her have it. She's a loser anyway – it's the only thing she has to look forward to.'

That was when the world before my eyes tilted dangerously.

Ten

The next thing I knew, I was standing outside the head's office with Lou, as Mr Winch disappeared inside. Our head teacher was known as 'the Sergeant', because of her cropped grey hair that looked like a helmet, and her no-nonsense approach to life. When Mr Winch went inside, Lou and I stared helplessly at the floor, and I tried my best not to be sick. I knew that I'd done something terrible to her, but I didn't dare look up to find out what it was.

I'd never been inside the Sergeant's office, but I'd heard plenty of rumours about people who'd ended up there. Once I'd overheard one of the Year Elevens in the canteen saying that she'd given him lunchtime detention every day for three weeks and he was made to clear rubbish from the netball courts in the freezing cold. She also made sure that he rang his parents in front of her to tell them what he'd done, and he was grounded for the rest of the year. There was no joking with the Sergeant.

It seemed as if hours passed as the two of us stood outside the heavy oak door with its old-fashioned brass handle. I was only vaguely aware of the noise of lessons going on in classrooms around us, and Lou hiccupping nervously next to me and wiping her eyes.

Finally, Mr Winch appeared and ushered us in.

As I'd expected, there was an impeccable sense of order in the Sergeant's office. She and Aunty Lyn would get on like a house on fire.

At one end of the room was a dark wooden desk, on which rested folders and papers arranged in neat piles, not a page out of place. The two screens of her computer were placed at what looked like an exact forty-five degree angle from one another, and out of the corner of my eye, I caught the glimmer of a gold-nibbed fountain pen, lying in its special velvet green holder. I could imagine the Sergeant grabbing it in her thick fingers and swiftly signing letters about detentions and exclusions. I tried to block that idea from my mind.

I sat in one of the perfect leather chairs, the seat dented by the weight of many bodies.

Lou and Mr Winch perched on the edge of a cream sofa opposite me, each staring at different spots on the carpet. Its pattern swirled beneath our feet, creating a horrid dizziness in my head. What had I done? I tried to catch Lou's eye and eventually she looked up at me. Her face was still flushed. She looked scared, and I felt awful. I mouthed the words, 'I'm sorry,' but she deliberately turned away.

The Sergeant leaned against her desk, her fingers linked. Close up, she looked younger, but no less scary than I'd anticipated.

'What happened? Facts. All I want is facts. No emotions. Just facts.'

'Isabel pushed Louise and she fell backwards into the costume room and hit her head,' said Mr Winch succinctly.

A gasp escaped my throat.

The Sergeant's beady eyes peered down at me.

'Isabel? What on earth were you thinking?'

Lou had a purple bruise spreading across her upper right arm and a plum-shaped swelling on one side of her head. The costume room was several metres under the stage and she must have fallen on to something sharp, perhaps the edge of Mr Winch's desk. How had it happened? How was it that I completely didn't realise what I was doing?

'I'm sorry,' I mumbled.

One of the Sergeant's dark eyebrows disappeared under the helmet of hair. I couldn't read her expression.

'Why did you do it?'

'I don't know. I wasn't... I wasn't thinking.'

'She was provoked by Louise,' Mr Winch offered, glancing over at Lou.

'What did you say to Isabel, Louise?

Lou flinched, but remained quiet. I saw the muscles of her back tense.

'She called Izzy a loser and said that she had nothing to look forward to,' Mr Winch reported accurately, when it was clear that Lou wasn't going to utter a word.

A deafening silence filled the room.

The Sergeant let out a long sigh. She picked up the fountain pen and rolled it between her fingers.

'Louise, are you badly hurt?' she asked finally.

'No,' said Lou, her lower lip trembling. But the guilt weighed even heavier on me, as I noticed that the purple bruise spread all the way to her elbow.

'Ask Nurse Cooper to check that you're OK and then you may return with Mr Winch to your lesson,' she snapped. 'Please come back and see me here at the end of the day. I feel there are a few things that you and I may need to discuss. In the meantime, I'm going to contact your mother.'

'Please could you not...' Lou began, but stopped midway through her sentence, seeing the Sergeant's glare. Her eyes bore into Lou's face, as if daring her to go on.

'You should have thought about that when you made your remark earlier, Louise.'

When the door shut behind them, I found myself edging deeper into the chair. For some reason, I wondered whether the Sergeant had any children of her own and if she did, whether they were scared of her too.

'I'm sorry,' I said. 'I shouldn't have pushed her. I don't know what came over me... I honestly didn't even know that I had...'

But then I heard the last three words I'd ever expect from her lips, 'Don't be sorry.'

'What?'

'You heard me. I don't normally say things like this. Don't be sorry for feeling the way you do. Yes, you shouldn't have lashed out at Louise, although she probably deserved it. Trust me, there will be many times in life when people say or do things to you and they deserve a reaction. Unfortunately, that doesn't give you permission to push or hit them. But you have every right to be angry... considering everything that's happened to you recently. You've dealt with it extremely bravely and it must be infuriating to have someone like Louise being nasty.'

My face was on fire. I sort of wanted her to shout at me, to give me a whole month's worth of detentions, to make me stand up in assembly and apologise for pushing Lou. Anything would have been better than this. But at last I understood - this strictest and most military of women had turned soft because she felt sorry for me.

'I'm all right.'

She continued to look at me, her nails tapping out a rhythm on the desk like tiny marching soldiers.

'Isabel, is this the first time that Louise has said something hurtful to you?' She was careful to hold my gaze.

'Yes,' I said, although of course that wasn't true. I just wanted the conversation to be over as soon as it possibly could be.

'If it happens again, I want you to report it directly to me, do you hear?'

'I will. Of course I will.'

'And... how are you doing generally?'

'Good,' I told her. It came out louder than I'd intended, although I'd tried my hardest to keep my voice calm.

'OK, Izzy. Go back to class.'

I nodded, still not quite believing I was getting off so lightly - no phone call to Dad, no letter to take home, nothing.

And then I was outside in the corridor once more, unsure of what to do next.

Eleven

I wandered about aimlessly. I couldn't face any more lessons. Not after the Lady Macbeth drama. So I went to the school office and told them I was sick. I wanted Dad to pick me up. I wanted to tell him everything - my nightmares, Lou, the mural, the mysterious colour thief and how all of what had happened had been my fault. Dad would understand and know what to do. I waited patiently for him to come to get me. He didn't.

Aunty Lyn came instead and made a massive fuss over me being unwell, checking how hot my forehead was.

'Where's Dad?' I asked her as soon as we were outside the school gates.

'He's at home, love. He's resting. He needs to rest at the moment. Sometimes I don't know whether it's better for him to be busy with his work or just to stop for a while. Anyway, he's already been to hospital. He'll be asleep now.'

I followed her to her car without a word, deliberately getting into the back, because I thought that would stop her asking as many questions as if I was sitting next to her. I soon realised that my tactic was useless.

'How was your day in general?' she asked, peering at me in the rear-view mirror.

'Fine.'

'And when did you start feeling bad?'

I wanted to say 'forty days and roughly four hours ago', but I didn't. Aunty Lyn didn't give up and continued to watch me in the mirror. She was looking at me so intently that I worried she wasn't paying attention to the road.

'Around midday,' I said eventually. 'Just after lunch. I felt sick, but I'll be OK.'

'Of course you will. You and your dad will both be OK. That doesn't make it any easier right now, though, does it?'

'Mhmm.' In situations like this, the shorter my answers were, the better.

'Hey, when I was dropping your dad off earlier, I bumped into Shelley, your friend Lou's mum.'

I gasped, but Aunty Lyn didn't notice. If she'd seen her in the morning, there was no way Shelley would have known what had happened in the auditions, but still I felt awfully nervous.

'What did she say?' I asked.

'She said she thought that you and Lou had fallen out and she figured that it was probably Lou's fault. I think she feels bad about it. She tried to explain that Lou's not very good at dealing with...'

'I don't care,' I snapped, so suddenly that Aunty Lyn's right leg jerked, causing her to brake and the driver behind to honk his horn. Neither of us said another word until we pulled up outside our house.

I stared out of the window at the spectral trees, their autumn leaves, clusters of reds and oranges, hanging on for dear life in the run-up to winter. My eyes settled on a pair of birds, swooping in V-shaped black patterns against the sky.

At home, Milo greeted me by jumping all over me and yelping.

'Has he been taken out for a walk?' I asked Aunty Lyn.

'He's had a run around the garden. Truth be told, I haven't had time today, Izzy. I did the shopping, then took...'

'Can I take him now?' I interrupted. I knew exactly where I wanted to go.

'You're not feeling well. Why don't you have a lie down and I'll make you some peppermint tea to settle your stomach? You can always take him out later when you're feeling better.'

Drat. I'd completely forgotten about the lie.

'I'm feeling much better than I was,' I improvised. 'I could use some fresh air.'

She looked at me hesitantly and sighed.

'Oh, well, if you think so... just take him for a short walk. Don't be long, mind, and take your key in case we've left the house before you're back. I'm taking your dad to the doctor at three o'clock.'

'To the doctor? What's wrong with him? Tell me,' I demanded. 'Is he ill?'

'He's not physically ill, Isabel. He's just been feeling very under the weather, as I'm sure you know. I believe that seeing the doctor will help him. Honestly it will,' she said, her voice wavered a bit. 'I was thinking I'd make meatballs later. You always loved meatballs when you came round to ours. Would you like them for dinner tonight?'

'Yeah, that would be good,' I said. I grabbed my keys from the bowl, put on Milo's lead and the moment that I was out of the door again, I felt better. I was worried about Dad of course but if he and Aunty Lyn were so preoccupied I certainly wasn't going to tell them about what had happened in school.

I headed straight for Toby's.

A woman with blonde, spiky hair answered. A galaxy of freckles dusted her cheeks. 'You must be Izzy. I'm Anna, Toby's mum. Toby's told me all about you. Come in. He's just in the back room doing some of his schoolwork.'

She patted Milo on the head and said nothing about him having to stay outdoors. I immediately liked her.

'Do you fancy something to eat or a cup of tea?'

'I'm OK, thanks.'

'Sorry, the kitchen's an absolute mess. We've been doing biology today and looking into the structure of cells. We've been creating a human cell and a plant cell from different things around the house, most of which ended up being kitchen ingredients.'

'Hi,' said Toby, emerging from what I guessed was his bedroom. I noticed something red and wobbly on his lap. 'It's a red blood cell,' he announced. 'More specifically a giant, edible red blood cell. It's made out of jelly. Did you know that red blood cells don't have a nucleus?'

'Very good,' replied Anna. 'And why are they important?'

'They carry oxygen around the body. And the average human has about thirty trillion of them. That's mad, isn't it? There's just so much red inside the human body.' His words caused a sudden bolt of panic in my stomach. They'd triggered a memory.

'There is,' Anna agreed. 'And also many other colours. Purple organs, veins that appear blue, skin that comes in a variety of different shades... The human body is quite literally filled with colour.'

'Can you come out to walk Milo?' I asked Toby.

'Yes. I'll finish this later,' he said. 'I promise I'll help to clear up. We just need to make sure that Spike is OK.'

'You can check in on him,' said Anna. 'But, Toby...'
'Mmm?'

'Please don't go into the river again. You were really lucky last time. I've heard the current there can be pretty bad. Keep Milo on the lead so he doesn't escape. You need to look out for each other.'

'We will, don't worry.'

'Your mum's awesome. You know that?' I said as we got outside.

'Yeah, she's pretty great. I probably don't tell her that enough.'

That made me think. Because, really, my own mum was the same. I never knew exactly what she was thinking and I loved that about her. There were people who would tell her that she shouldn't be doing her job at the school because it was too stressful, and it didn't pay very much. Nanna Jem would go on and on about it.

This one time she did it, I'd imagined Mum would

laugh it off and change the subject like she usually did (she never liked being too serious for long), but she'd stopped what she was doing and given Nanna a look.

'Do you think I would be doing it if I didn't love it?' Nanna had been strangely shocked by the reply. She didn't mention it again.

The memory made me certain Toby would love Mum. They would get on amazingly well. I was on the verge of asking him whether he would like to meet her, but somehow I couldn't.

Maybe it was because I was jealous that he could tell his mum everything. Anna already knew Milo's name and everything about Spike. Toby must have told her about his rescue mission, even though he knew it would probably make her doubly worried. I hadn't told Dad anything – at least not in detail. I wanted to, but he was always at the hospital when I needed to speak to him, and when he wasn't, his thoughts were so full of Mum that there was no room for anything else. Even though there was nothing he could do. There was nothing *we* could do.

As we made our way down the alleyway to the river, the feeling of not being able to do anything grew and grew in my head. 'I've been feeling so good about Spike, but now all of a sudden, I've started to worry,' I admitted to Toby. 'He's so weak and helpless. And with the whole Milo rescue, we didn't even have a chance to give him his food.'

'He *was* weak,' Toby answered. 'But you can't automatically assume that he won't make it.'

He sounded mad and I was so surprised that I paused mid-step.

'Are you OK?'

'Yeah,' he mumbled. 'Why wouldn't I be? After all, it's only what other people think of me.'

'Of you?' I didn't understand.

'It's easy to just guess I won't be able to do stuff. But I can - a lot more than you would ever expect. I could have chosen an electric-powered chair, but instead I push myself around, don't I? It took me ages to build up the strength to do it, but I did. I push even when I get muddy, or my shoulders hurt, or I can't carry the stuff I want to carry. Yeah, I need help sometimes, but so does everyone. Spike needs help at the moment, but that doesn't mean that he'll never be able to look after himself.'

He started wheeling fast down the river path. For a frightening moment, the wheelchair bounced over a stone and I thought I'd see Toby flying through the air towards the water. Luckily, it balanced itself and came to a stop, the wheels lodging in the mud of the bank.

'Are you crazy?' I shouted. 'What did your mum

just say? Why are you racing ahead like a maniac? You could have landed in the river!'

I could see the shock on Toby's face. He knew it had been a close shave.

'Sorry... sorry,' he said. 'I still sometimes forget that I can't run away when I want to.'

I sat down in the open end of the van and looked at him. I thought about him in the wheelchair, unable to move his legs.

'I can't understand what it's like,' I said. 'I can't even try. And I know that you must think it's horribly unfair. But I know you're more than able to do stuff. The wheelchair didn't stop you rescuing Milo, did it? I don't think I'd have been able to do that. I said that stuff about Spike because sometimes I feel like *I* can't really do anything - *I* can't change anything.'

I wanted to swallow my words as soon as I'd said them. How could I even say something like that to somebody in Toby's position?

He just smiled at me - a sad smile.

'I almost wish I hadn't known what it was like... you know, before.'

His blue eyes blinked behind his glasses and for the first time he didn't look as bold and fearless as usual. It made me like him even more.

'Do you really? If that were true, you would be an

entirely different person. You might not be here with me now...'

At this point, Milo, bored of being restrained on his lead, leaped into Toby's lap, and settled himself down.

'Sorry for acting like such an idiot,' he said eventually, giving me a half-smile.

'It's OK. Shall we look for Spike, then?' I hoped our favourite cygnet would be alive and well.

We had a look in the spot where we'd last seen the mother and father along with four of the cygnets. There was no sign of them.

'Do you think they might have moved to another part of the river?'

'Maybe, but it's more likely that they're searching for food. If they are, I don't think they could've gone very far.'

'Why don't I go that way?' I said, pointing. 'And you and Milo can go that way? Only go as far as the bridge, and if you don't find them, meet me back here.'

'Good plan.'

Annoyingly, a light drizzle had started which made it more difficult to search - the water, the grassy bank, the sky, all blurred like a painting in which the colours had run.

I detected a movement of white across the cold grey surface of the water. The parent swans! They were there, closely trailed by four of their offspring. I edged closer and saw that Spike wasn't part of the group. I gave him the benefit of the doubt, thinking he might just be lagging behind the others, but there was no sign of any other bobbing little head.

My eyes scanned the horizon for a few more minutes and then I began walking back. Toby wasn't at our meeting spot, so I sat on the bank to wait. I couldn't stop my hands shaking in my lap.

Then, suddenly, I spotted him close to the river's edge.

'Izzy! Come here. Look! Milo found him. He's hiding in the grass.' And there he was. Shivering and bewildered, but still very much alive, Spike had nestled between two clumps of grass. He'd cleverly chosen a position that shielded him against the wind. I breathed out – a long, grateful breath. It took me a few moments to remember about the bag of lettuce in my pocket and I pulled it out straightaway, gently throwing some into the water next to him. I motioned for Milo to stay quiet, though strangely enough he didn't need telling. He lay down obediently on the riverbank, watching proceedings.

A minute or so passed before the baby swan made up his mind to begin eating. He struggled at first, his tiny throat constricting, but soon he managed to break the lettuce into small enough pieces to swallow.

'They're coming back,' Toby whispered. I glanced up to see the mother swan reappear with the rest of her brood. She was carrying something in her beak. Before I could see what it was, one of the cygnets snatched it from her.

When she got within reaching distance of Spike, she attempted again to get the last bit of food to him by putting her beak right next to his, but there was a flutter of feathers and one of Spike's siblings intervened. All of a sudden, Milo jumped up and began to bark at the greedy cygnet, frightening him away.

'Calm down!' I shouted at him, but the intervention gave Spike the chance to at least finish what he was eating.

'He's standing up for him,' Toby said, grinning as he ruffled Milo's ears. 'This means we're going to have to keep coming back to make sure that he's fed, at least until he grows stronger and can fend for himself. We've got everything we need now. And you know what else?'

'What?'

'Swans are incredibly clever. I read that they recall who's been kind to them, so hopefully he'll recognise us each time we come.'

'You're such a swan geek,' I told him, though I secretly hoped that he was right.

We checked that the fishing rod was carefully stowed away in the van along with our two bags of lettuce. I tucked them in the corner so that if it rained, it wouldn't go soggy. As we made our way up the bank, I was already looking forward to coming back again tomorrow.

Twelve

I felt a cold rush of air. The shadow and smoke cleared and I was lifted in a single jerking motion by a pair of strong hands. I could clearly see the skin – soft, leathery brown. I knew who the hands belonged to. The shadow man. The colour thief. I tried to twist from his grasp, but he forced something over my face. It was cool and smooth, like a glass mask.

My coughing came in short bursts and my lungs filled with a furious, raging red. I could feel it flowing in my lungs, threatening to escape through my throat. I struggled against him with all the force I could muster. I wouldn't let him steal the red. I wouldn't let it go. I kicked out madly and still he forced the mask on to my face, fastening it tightly, so that it didn't move.

5.54 a.m.

My breathing took a long time to return to normal. I climbed out of bed and crept to the window. There was no moon over the river and the world lay shrouded in misty darkness. I could just about make out the outline of our van. I thought of the beetles that scuttled through the back of it, and I thought of Spike and Toby. I put my hand on my chest and focused on nothing but breathing regularly in and out, in and out. Even though it was still dark, I knew what I had to do next. I couldn't stop myself. I picked up the little torch I always kept on my bedside table and shone it on the mural. I saw the theft straightaway. I was surprised at my relief that it wasn't red. The red of my Juliet lips was still there, as was the red of Mum's nightie in the photo of us at the hospital. It was only her hair that was no longer brown. It hung in limp, white strands around her face, making her ghost-like. The crawling began in my stomach as I counted the colours left. Purple, red and black. I couldn't let him take red. That much I knew. When red and purple were gone, there would only be the washed-out emptiness of the Blackest Day.

I dared myself to make the small circle of light illuminate our first proper holiday as a family - skiing in the Alps, where the trees on the side of the mountain were now so white that they merged with the snow. Mum had been proud of her French and thought that she'd communicated really well with the woman who ran the ski school, but somehow, aged seven, I'd ended up in the advanced group, having never skied before in my life. There I was on the wall in my oversized jacket and hat doing a very wobbly snow-plough all the way down the mountain.

From that holiday, my main memory was of losing my ski on the chairlift, and Mum and Dad both trudging through the snow with me for hours trying to find it. When I closed my eyes, I could still feel the frozen flakes that had fallen into the tops of my boots.

I could see the blue ski unclipping from my boot and hurtling in ever-expanding circles through the air, way into the white depths below.

Then the memory came to an abrupt close and, no matter how hard I tried, I couldn't figure out whether or not I'd got the ski back.

Had we managed to find it, or did we have to get a new pair from the local hire centre? I closed my eyes. I delved deep into my memory. My tired brain refused to cooperate. Who could tell me? The only person was Dad. He would know. I stopped, hesitating in the doorway. Would he be mad at me? I hadn't been back to the hospital, even though I knew he was hoping that I would. Then I remembered what he'd said to me the other day about being 'specsational', so I tiptoed across the hall and knocked softly on his door. There was no answer. I quietly slipped inside.

Dad's curtains were open and the light from the street lamp fell over his bed. He was lying in the middle, a lonely island in a sea of duvet. The room smelled of Aunty Lyn's favourite floral washing powder.

I sat on the edge of the bed and pulled back the covers. Dad stirred and one of his eyes opened. I stifled a laugh. When I was really little I would come into my parents' bedroom in the middle of the night and demand that they read to me. Dad would pretend not to hear, but he wouldn't be able to resist opening one beady eye. His reaction was exactly the same now.

'Diz?'

'Did I find the ski?'

He propped himself up on his elbows and I could see him looking at me in the sliver of light from the street lamp. I waited for him to ask what I was talking about but there was only a moment of hesitation before his mouth stretched into a grin. 'Yep, we found it. It took hours and hours and I was ready to give up, but you insisted that we weren't going back to the chalet without it. You didn't know how to use the button lift. Remember when your legs were dangling in the air? You looked like one of those cartoons of a girl attached to a balloon.'

'And you had to grab me?'

'Exactly.' He rubbed his eyes. 'What time is it, Diz? Why are you up so early?'

'I couldn't sleep. And then I couldn't remember what had happened.'

'Ah, I see… It would have come to you. Memory often catches up later.'

'I know, but I wanted to be sure. Dad?'

'Yeah, Diz?'

'Have you given up on Project Elephant?'

'Given up? Of course not. There are so many animals out there I haven't even met yet and that need my help. I'm hoping you might even come with me one day.'

'Maybe I will…'

I could see his eyes drooping again when I suddenly burst out, 'Dad – I'm sorry.'

'What for?'

It was a good question. There was so much I was sorry for that I was bursting with it. And even if I tried to put it into words for Dad, I knew I wouldn't be able to.

'That I don't visit Mum every day. I just… I can't…'

'I know, sshh. It's all right. It's not easy. You need to do things in your own time.'

I was closer than ever to telling him everything, to asking him about the colour thief. Dad would know what to do, and he would know how to stop him. But his eyes were properly closed now and within moments he was fast asleep.

I tucked the duvet around him and slowly crept back to my own room.

'How are you feeling this morning?' Aunty Lyn asked. 'Did you sleep OK?' She was still in her pyjama bottoms and an oversized jumper, and without make-up her face looked different – softer.

'Mmm.' I'd woken up to the sound of clanging glass from downstairs.

'Sorry about the racket, but I wanted to get all of this out before the bin men come.' She was dragging stacks of recycling bags through the front door, double bagging some of them to prevent the contents spilling everywhere. The stench was horrible. Milo was busy running round sniffing each bag in turn.

'Would you mind giving me a hand, Izzy? Take some of the smaller bags, would you?'

I picked up three at once, which was probably too many, but I forced myself to drag them into the front garden. The weeds had disappeared and Aunty Lyn had mowed the lawn. Even the lavender bush that Mum had planted was neatly clipped. She would have been happy to see it so well looked after.

'Where did this come from?' I asked, pointing to the bags.

'The back garden. Didn't you notice the smell? You had about eight bin bags there and nobody had taken them out for the collection.'

She wiped her hands on a dishcloth and changed the subject.

'I popped out and got us some chocolate twists for breakfast. I thought you'd like them. Hattie and Mick always insist on at least one a week. Mind you, they're probably having more now that I'm not there every day to monitor their diet. But they've got all these mock exams so they deserve a treat.'

She opened the fridge, which had been scrubbed clean, not a hairy carrot in sight.

'You probably should be there with them...' I said, suddenly guilty about the amount of time that she had spent with us.

'They'll be fine with Uncle Tom and I want to be here with you for now,' she answered simply. 'I'm going to take these bottles to the bottle bank. I thought I could give you a lift to school on the way if you're sure that you want to go in today?'

The bottles were lined up on the kitchen table, rows

and rows of them like a small glass army. Some were tall, clear wine bottles, but most were small with a brown tint. They were a reminder of the most recent of the colour disappearances on my mural. I climbed the stairs to pack my bag and surveyed the wall. In the light of day, the absence of brown was even starker. Combined with green, its disappearance had caused a change in weather – everything that was lush and spring-like looked as if it had turned to winter. I moved close to the wall then, peering at it from just a few centimetres away. And the more I stared, the more I realised the colour was still there, although only the very faintest traces. It was as if somebody had dabbed at it with a sponge, intent on stealing its energy and spirit. But why? Why did the colour thief want my colours?

I would definitely ask Dad tonight. I had put it off for long enough.

A shrill whistle pierced the air. I hurried over to the window and saw Toby waving at me from the riverbank. I couldn't quite make out his expression, but I sensed that he was excited.

Aunty Lyn was still outside when I came downstairs, attempting unsuccessfully to fit all the bottles into the recycling bin.

'I'm going to walk,' I told her. 'Thanks for offering to drive me, but it won't take long.'

I went quickly down the alleyway to the river and over the bridge. The mud squelched around my newly cleaned school shoes and by the time I reached Toby, I could already feel the tell-tale signs of damp on my toes.

'What's up?' I asked him.

'Nothing,' he said. 'It was just that I found these in the garage yesterday.' He indicated a box of logs balancing on his lap. 'I thought we could build Spike a shelter. I've been worrying about how he's doing when we're not there, and I figured he's probably not so safe on the open water while he's still tiny. This is what I thought we could do.' He showed me a sketch of what at first glance looked like a small house, complete with a veranda.

'It would only be about this size,' he said, spreading his arms to slightly more than the width of his knees. 'The roof would give him a bit of shelter, and we could put some straw inside, in case he gets cold.'

'Where would you put it?'

'That's what I came out here to figure out. You see that bit of land that juts out under the bridge? I think maybe that would be a good spot.'

'The current's strong there, though. What about putting it here? We could wedge it in above the water, between these two branches. It's where we saw him

105

first, and he always seems to come back here for his food,' I said, pointing to Spike's bush.

Toby considered it for a moment. Then he passed me two of the bigger logs.

'See if they're long enough for us to use as a base,' he instructed me. I scrambled carefully down the bank. I almost, almost made it…

I fell on my bum with a thud, but then I heard Toby chuckle, and pleasant warmth spread through my stomach. Before I knew it, I was laughing so hard that I could barely lift myself back up.

'You're completely caked!' he yelled, as I finally managed to make it to the bush. I laid the logs between two of the biggest branches – they were perfect.

I climbed back up the bank and handed them to Toby, who was still doubled over in his chair chuckling.

'I wish I'd filmed you, Izzy! Oh, it was priceless; absolutely priceless!'

'Shut up,' I said to him, although he'd set me off again. Then I looked at my watch, and saw that I didn't even have enough time to get changed. I swung my rucksack on to my muddy back, and legged it, telling Toby that I would meet him after school.

In the few minutes left before the bell, I tried to wash off the worst of the mud in the loos. It was hopeless. I managed to get most of it off my shoes, and I took off my jumper and rolled it up in a ball in my bag, but there wasn't much I could do about the back of my skirt.

I was so worried about being muddy that at first I thought it must be the cause of the sudden silence when I walked into the classroom. It was as if somebody had just turned off the sound in a film. Even Mona and Harpreet looked down at their desks and avoided my gaze when I said hello.

One of the boys in the back row shouted out, 'And the winner of Round One enters the arena. The question on everyone's lips is: when's the rematch and who will come away victorious? I'll be taking bets this lunchtime, folks. Roll up!' It was then that the real reason for the silence sank in and the spiders went mad in my stomach.

Lou was sitting in her usual seat, a team of devoted friends gathered round her. She had a large white bandage stuck to the side of her head. *Get Well Soon* cards were arranged in an elaborate display in front of her.

I sat down, trying my hardest not to look in her direction, and saw a note on my desk. On the front was a tiny cartoon picture of a man reading a newspaper.

PTO it said at the bottom. On the reverse the same man was scrunching the newspaper and aiming it through a basketball hoop.

Below it was written:

It will be old news tomorrow.

Frank looked at me and grinned reassuringly. The spiders settled instantly.

Thirteen

We had art first and I was thankful that Lou wasn't in the same class. Mr Leah asked us if anyone had guessed his riddle. I knew, of course, but I didn't feel like drawing attention to myself. Jonah answered. He got the name wrong, pronouncing it 'Dally', but Mr Leah let it go.

'Dalí often described his paintings as "hand-painted dream photographs",' he said. 'So, for your next project, I would like you to use a dream as your source of inspiration. I won't say anything more than that. You'll have five double-lessons in which to work on this, so really think it through carefully; maybe even consider doing a few rough sketches first. I'm going to hand out some A3 paper - you can use charcoal, poster paint, oil paint, or anything else you can find in the room.'

I sat in front of my sheet, allowing my stubby pencil to flick slowly through the fingers of my left hand. At first my mind was as blank as the paper, but then

I noticed the cans of spray paint, and I knew exactly what I was going to try. I'd seen Mum use this style for a portrait that she'd been commissioned to do. At first she'd only tested it, doubting that it would work, but it had ended up looking perfect. She'd somehow managed to create the picture half in spray-painted shadow and half in the light. The side of the woman's face that was exposed was so vividly drawn, that every vein and wrinkle was visible. I wanted to create the same sense of shadow, but I wasn't nearly as good as Mum. I used to be sad that I hadn't inherited her gift, but she would say, 'You're an amazing actress, Izzy. Don't be greedy - leave some talents for others.'

I didn't hold high hopes for my painting, but I would give it a go. I took the yellow can first and let loose on the page. I held it close to one edge to achieve a strong colour effect, and then moved it further away so that by the time it reached the other side, it was so faint that it was barely there. Then I did the same with blue, brown and purple, the colours bleeding into a wild cloud of smoke. Finally, I grabbed a stick of charcoal and began to draw the outline of a figure emerging from the haze. His head first - a dark, smudged, shadowy oval - two outstretched arms, the fingers curling, as if to grasp something, I was so engrossed that I didn't even notice Frank had perched himself on the other end of my work bench. I glanced over and saw that, like me, he'd done no sketching or planning and had gone straight for the paints. He'd brought over a whole box of them and seemed to be opening pots randomly.

At last he selected black, dipped his paintbrush in, and swirled it vigorously around the page, the tip of his tongue at the side of his mouth with the effort of creating a single continuous loop.

'It's a vortex,' he said. 'I keep having this dream where I'm paragliding and I go really high into the air, above the clouds, and then suddenly *schwooop* – I get sucked into this vortex – like a black hole – and I go catapulting into it, thousands of miles per hour and these zombies appear from nowhere and start chasing me, so I run like mad...'

He demonstrated by hurling himself halfway across the classroom, bouncing off the back wall, then skidding in my direction. I stepped away quickly, narrowly avoiding a collision.

'Steady on,' said Mr Leah, grinning. 'This is impressive, Frank. I can really see the movement in your picture, even before you demonstrated it. I like the impact of black on white, but maybe you could add a bit of texture to show the things, or the fragments of things that are being sucked into the vortex? Look, you could use some of the netting here...'

He handed the sheet of wire to Frank and then stopped suddenly in front of my picture. I was just smudging the charcoal, carefully blending the shadow man into the colours around him.

I felt the weight of Mr Leah's gaze. I wished that he would move on and comment on someone else's work, but his feet remained fixed to the spot.

'What is it, Izzy?' he asked.

'I'm not quite finished.'

'No, I can see that, but I'm intrigued. What is the title of your work?'

'*The Colour Thief,*' I replied, without thinking.

He looked at me, a puzzled expression on his face.

'A fascinating name. And... how are you doing?' he asked more quietly.

'The same,' I said. I felt myself growing hot.

'Well, if you ever feel that you'd like to talk about anything, you know where to find me. And you know that it's usually quiet in here at lunchtime, so if you wanted to come and do some more work on this and have a chat, I'll be here.'

'Thank you,' I mumbled. 'But I have nothing to talk about...'

I was first into the biology lab. I sat by myself at the back, as far away as possible from Lou, who took a prime spot on the front bank of desks. My night of broken sleep was catching up with me. I felt exhausted and my eyes drooped in the heat of the lab. Before I knew it, I'd dozed off. I dreamed of somebody whose face I couldn't quite see, who took my painting and ran it under the tap until the colours merged into an ugly grey sludge and disappeared down the sink.

I was tugging at the person's arm to make them stop when I heard nervous laughter. I opened my eyes to see twenty-four faces watching me closely.

'Turn around,' said Mrs Yen impatiently. 'There's nothing to see.' My face burned with shame. Jemima sniggered and muttered something to Lou.

'I want you to get into pairs and start planning your demographics project,' Mrs Yen continued, battling the chatter. 'You can choose what you want to survey, be it eye colour, hair colour, shoe size or anything else. On your posters, I'd like to see a summary of what causes variations in your demographic and then you can use the class as your sample to see the spread of difference.'

'Maybe we'll do a spread of how dangerous people are,' I heard Lou whisper loudly, as she glanced in my direction.

'Louise, I would appreciate if you stuck to the subject,

please, and stopped talking nonsense. You have the rest of the lesson to start planning with your partner and then we'll continue next week.'

There was a buzz of activity as everyone got into pairs. I turned to Mona, who was sitting closest to me, but she'd already paired up with Harpreet. To my left, a pair of boys had also coupled off. It didn't take me long to figure out that there was an odd number of us in the class and I was the one left out.

Mrs Yen noticed and came over immediately.

'Izzy, join Mona and Harpreet. You can be a three,' she said. But the moment she walked away, the girls looked at me, scared expressions on their faces.

'Why don't we do two projects?' suggested Mona. 'You work on a separate thing, Izzy, and then we can just put them together in one poster. We'll leave you a space.'

I didn't understand.

'That's just more to do, though. Why don't you want to work together on it?' I asked.

They looked shiftily at each other. 'Well, it would just be easier because… what if you get angry and…'

'And what?' My face felt so hot that I thought it might melt.

'Lou said that it's best not to say anything to you… in case, you know… you lash out,' Harpreet explained.

I looked at the floor. The squares of lino danced before my eyes. I leaned my hand on the desk to steady myself.

'Izzy, are you... are you OK?' I heard Mona ask. And then suddenly I found myself on my feet, walking swiftly in the direction of the door, past Mrs Yen who had her back turned, writing something on the whiteboard, through the dimly lit corridor of the science block with its rows of lab coat hooks, past the netball courts and school office. As it was still the middle of the lesson, nobody was around and so nobody spotted me. It would be a good fifteen minutes before anyone in my class realised that I wasn't coming back.

I walked right through the main doors next to the school office and through the front gates. Within moments I was on the street and still my feet moved in a steady, marching rhythm. *Left, right, left, right.*

I walked instinctively in the direction of the park, breaking into a jog and then into a wild run.

I ran all the way down Gulliver Avenue, passing ghostly trees on either side, their branches open to the wind. I pushed through clusters of office workers at the zebra crossing, past Mr Joshi's corner shop with the fruit bowls lined up outside, the ripe plums, the shiny apples, and into Jamieson Park. I only stopped when I reached the water fountain. I leaned on its edge, breathing fast.

I turned to see whether I'd been followed, but there was nobody familiar in sight.

The park was empty apart from a group of mums with their young children sitting on rugs arranging a picnic. One of the women took off her jacket and stretched her arms, enjoying the weather. I saw a glimmer of brightness seeping through a gap in the pale, pale sky and realised that it was a clear, sunny day.

I strolled past the playground and the tennis courts, staring down at my shoes as I walked. I'd thought I was moving forwards without aim or agenda, but when I arrived at our favourite spot, I wasn't surprised to find myself there. My feet must have known where they were heading.

The building was completely overgrown now. People used to say that it would be redeveloped in the summer, then next year, then the year after, but nothing ever happened. Mum and I had found it completely by accident, when we went searching for lost tennis balls. It was hidden behind a tall hedge, old scaffolding still surrounding the dirty brick. I think it used to have *Danger* signs on it, but even those had fallen off or rotted away.

I was almost too big for the hole in the hedge now. Either it had closed up or I was bigger. I squeezed through, burrowing my hands in the earth. Swarms of ants scurried away. Twigs scratched the exposed skin on the back of my neck. I felt a sudden mad panic that I wouldn't get through – that I would be stuck somewhere nobody would look for me. I propelled myself forwards but my legs stuck in the hedge, my shoelaces caught. I kicked fiercely till the laces snapped, and pulled with all my strength. On the other side, I stood, dirty and out of breath in front of the derelict building, which seemed not to have changed since the last time that I'd been here – long, long before the Blackest Day.

Mum and I used to sit in this very spot, pretending to be rich ladies from Victorian times, sipping tea from dainty teacups and being served neatly cut sandwiches by our butler. Sometimes, when it was sunny, we would bring a picnic, paper and paints. I would mess around, drawing whatever came into my head, but Mum would draw detailed pictures of the old house, taking the utmost care over every brick.

I stared at the exact view that she'd painted. I wanted to remember – what she'd said, the smell of the tubes of acrylic scattered on the grass, the sharp tang of the cheese and ketchup sandwiches. I sat for what could have been minutes or could have been hours, but nothing came back to me. Nothing, except that flicker of an image of the two of us there.

I gave up when I noticed it was getting dark. When

I checked my watch I couldn't believe it was almost six o'clock. I pulled myself back through the hole in the hedge, and ran through the empty park to the gate.

When I reached Gulliver Avenue, the street lamps were shining.

'Izzy! Wait a sec, love!'

I ground to a halt and spun around. Lou's mum waved to me from the door of Mr Joshi's shop. Just my luck. I wished I hadn't stopped. I wished I'd pretended not to have heard her. She was beckoning me. It seemed she was alone. I waited patiently for her to finish paying for her shopping, praying that Dad hadn't freaked out and sent a search party for me.

'Thanks for waiting,' said Shelley. 'Did your dad get my voicemail?' She sounded worried.

'Voicemail?'

'Yes. I tried to ring a couple of times since... since what happened between you and Lou the other day.' In the glow cast by the street lamp, I couldn't quite make out her expression. This was it. I felt my face instantly heating up. Of course she would tell Dad and Aunty Lyn. I wouldn't be able to keep it from them any longer.

'I'm sorry...' I began, but she stopped me by putting a hand on my shoulder.

'I don't want to hear it,' she said. 'Louise shouldn't have said what she said. She can be thoughtless and downright awful at times. I was ashamed of how she behaved. I've spoken to her, Izzy, and told her that she must apologise to you.'

I stared at Shelley, unblinking. Her hand felt heavy on my shoulder, but she didn't move it away, as if frightened that the minute she let go, I would be off.

'Thank you,' I managed, breaking the horrible silence.

'Don't thank me, Izzy. I couldn't do anything... I saw and I couldn't do anything...' she whispered. I knew then that she wasn't talking about what Lou had done, but about something very different, and I couldn't listen any more. I wrenched myself free and ran down the road, faster than I've ever run before.

Fourteen

The door swung open before I'd managed to turn the key.

'Izzy! She's here! Oh, thank goodness.'

Dad's stubbly face collapsed with relief. He hugged me so tight that he almost knocked us both over.

'Oh, thank goodness,' he repeated over and over into my hair.

'Izzy!' cried Aunt Lyn, emerging from the kitchen. She was clutching her notebook with her phone balanced between her ear and shoulder.

'She's here, Anna... No, don't worry. We'll ring you back...' she said into the phone.

Her voice shook - I wasn't sure whether it was from anger or relief.

'Izzy, where were you? We got a call from the school and we've been driving the streets looking for you for hours. Anna and Toby went out separately to see if you were by the river... We all thought something awful must have happened. I was honestly about to ring the police.'

I could see that she was on the verge of tears. I almost wished that they would both start shouting, but they just stood there, waiting patiently for an explanation.

'Where did you go, Izzy? Where were you?' Dad sat me down at the kitchen table and paced the room, rubbing both hands across his face.

'I... Stuff at school's been terrible recently. And today something... something happened and I couldn't stand it any longer. So I left the lesson... I just walked out and I went to the park.'

Dad stared at me, as if trying to read my expression.

'Izzy, what's going on?' he asked finally. 'I got an odd voicemail from Lou's mum the other day. I didn't call back, because I didn't know what she was talking about, but I think you do. You know you can...' Dad began, but Aunty Lyn interrupted him.

'Why didn't you tell anyone where you were going? Surely you knew that we would be worried sick? Don't you think that your poor dad has enough to be worrying about?'

Their barrage of questions hit me from all sides. A pulse was beating faster and faster in my head. And then the words came spilling out of my mouth before my brain had a chance to catch up.

'I don't care!' I yelled. 'I DON'T CARE!'

'Izzy!' Dad shouted after me, but I legged it upstairs, slamming my bedroom door shut.

I sat down shaking. My face in its different forms stared back at me from above my bed: newborn-Izzy, toddler-Izzy, skiing-Izzy, Juliet-Izzy, Izzy-on-the-day-Milo-joined-our-family... The bubbles of anger continued to burst in my head. Not only was it all colourless and empty now, but in this careful documentation of my life, there was one horrid moment that was missing.

I scrabbled desperately in my desk drawers and grabbed a thick black marker pen that I'd last used to label boxes of stuff I wanted to put in the attic. I took off the lid. Then I walked up to the most recent picture of myself and put the marker down hard to the right of it, where the next scene should have gone. My hand moved wildly, frantically covering every centimetre of wall I could reach. Black scribbles erupted, spilling into millions of tiny cobwebs, and still I carried on.

The finished product was a thick, spreading cloud of darkness. I'd used up all the ink in the pen and I was exhausted, but satisfied. *That* day was finally documented on the wall. The mural was up to date.

I crumpled to the floor and saw the warm, dark

space under the bed beside me. I rolled into it, tucking my knees into my chest, among the clouds of dust.

I don't know how long I lay there before a voice reached me through the haze of my anger.

'Izzy! Izzy? Can I come in?'

It was Toby. I stayed quiet. I didn't want to be disturbed. Not now.

'Izzy, I know you're in there,' he persisted. 'Can you come down?'

I heard the clank of his wheels moving across the kitchen lino, a sudden bark and a rustling noise. I visualised Milo jumping into his lap.

I heard Aunty Lyn say, 'I think we should leave her for a bit,'

'Izzy!' Toby called again. He wasn't one to give in.

I willed him to go away. But instead of the noise of the front door shutting, I heard a peculiar sound, somewhere between a thud and a drag.

'It's OK, I can do it,' he said, amid Aunty Lyn's protests.

I curled myself up even tighter, attempting the trick that Mum had taught me when I was very small, which would help me to calm down. I shut my eyes, and counted down from a hundred. My hiding place was suddenly boiling hot and I felt sticky beads of sweat on my forehead.

When I got to seventy-four, I heard the door being pushed open.

'You're horrendously stubborn, aren't you?'

'Toby.'

'Who else would it be? Didn't you hear me yelling at you from downstairs?'

'I did, but I... I didn't think you'd come up here.'

'I had to, because *you* wouldn't come down,' he said accusingly. 'The things I do for you.'

We lay in silence for a while. From my position, I could see his legs just to the side of the bed, and his long fingers tapping out a rhythm on the carpet.

'Coming out?' he asked casually.

'I can't.'

'OK, I suppose I'll have to come to you,' he said, pulling himself under the bed. I had to shuffle against the wall to make room for him.

'Eurgh, it's disgusting in here. It's like this place has never seen a vacuum.'

'You don't have to be here. Nobody asked you to come.' I rolled on to my side, away from him.

'Let's say I want to, even though you're being ridiculous.'

'Why?'

'Why? I don't know why you're being ridiculous. But if you're asking why I'm here - I just thought you might have something interesting to tell me.'

'I don't,' I snapped and then felt guilty for being so horrid. 'Do you have anything?'

'Anything...?'

'Anything interesting to tell *me*?'

He was silent for a minute, thinking.

'Biology OK?'

'I suppose.'

'Do you know how many bones there are in the human body?'

'Umm... I don't know. I would guess about one hundred and fifty?'

'Nope - two hundred and six in adults, but babies have more than two hundred and seventy when they're born.'

'How's that possible?' I asked, turning to face him.

'Some of them merge as you grow so you become stronger. D'you know how many bones in the spine?'

'Isn't it one big bone?'

'No, don't be stupid, otherwise how would you be able to bend? You'd be completely stiff. There are thirty-three small bones in the spine, but I only have thirty-two and a half.'

'How come?'

'Because of the accident.'

'Oh.' I could sense that we were coming to what Dad

would call 'the crux of the matter', but I couldn't tell whether Toby was ready to say any more about it yet. It turned out that he was.

'I know that you're curious and I don't mind telling you. It was awful. My own stupid fault. I was really into skateboarding at the time. I loved it almost as much as football. We were fed up of going to the local half-pipe.'

'Half-pipe?'

'Ramp. It's a semicircle. You know, you stand on the platforms on either side and then skate from one side to the other?'

'Oh, yeah, I know what you mean.'

'I was with my friend, Chai - we got bored because there were lots of little kids trying to butt in, so we decided to build our own. We found some old boards and bricks left over in Chai's garage from when his uncle was building an attic extension. First we tried to make a ramp in my back garden, but there wasn't enough room. Then I suggested that it would be great to create it on the garage roofs...'

He tailed off but I wanted to hear the rest.

'And then what?'

'Well, it was a long row of garages so we managed to build an awesome sort of wave. We lined the bricks up in three mountains and put the boards on top. They were quite flexible so they created a great sensation, almost as if you were surfing, on wheels. It was incredible – flying up and down through the air, seeing the rooftops of the houses around us.

'Anyway, first we linked the three peaks and it all worked really well and then Chai thought he would test it with four. It was still OK, but he landed pretty close to the edge of the roof at the other end. We should have noticed at that point that we'd made the ramp too long, but we didn't. So I gave it a go, just the way that he had, but maybe with a little bit more force.'

'You fell, didn't you?' I wanted to get to the moment before he did, and then I realised what I'd said and clamped my hand over my mouth. 'I'm sorry,' I muttered through my fingers.

'Yeah,' Toby said in his normal voice as if he was telling me a random piece of news.

'I'm sorry, I'm sorry,' I repeated, forcing my fists into my eyes. It made black floating dots appear before me, even in the dark.

'I flew through the air and I landed hard – incredibly hard – on my back. I felt the most insane pain, and then nothing, absolutely nothing, except the thump of my blood in my head.'

'Did you faint?'

'No, I was still conscious, and maybe my arms burned a bit because I'd grazed them, but the intense feeling in my back was gone. Chai came running over. I can still see the look on his face. He thought I'd died. He rang for the ambulance.'

'And what did they do? At the hospital?'

'So many different tests. I was there for days. Then the doctor told me that I'd shattered an intervertebral disc, which is basically a joint that allows movement between different bones in your spine. It caused a puncture in my spinal cord, which is part of my nervous system.'

The medical phrases swam through my brain.

'That's basically why I can't feel my legs,' he summarised, and for the first time ever his voice shook.

'When did it happen?'

'Just over a year ago. Last July. I didn't really want to go anywhere after that. I just stayed at home in bed. When I was half-asleep, I could sometimes pretend that it was just like before and that somehow I would open my eyes and be able to jump out of bed and run downstairs. I didn't want to see anyone and I definitely didn't want to go back to school...'

'And did you... go back?'

'I missed a bit of the start of term, but I went back. I soon found out that getting around wouldn't be easy because only some of the buildings in my old school had wheelchair access. And it took me a while to get used to always seeing people at their stomach level, rather than face-to-face.'

'What were your friends like about it?'

'Generally good, but, you know... it wasn't the same as before. And then the restaurant Mum worked in opened another sister restaurant here and she wanted to give it a go, you know - a fresh start.'

We lay together for a while in the thick, comfortable darkness.

'Do *you* want to tell *me* anything?'

'Yes,' I said. 'It's about a day. *That* day,' I corrected myself. 'The Blackest Day. But I can't... I can't tell you just yet.'

Fifteen

'*Can you hear me? Can you hear me?*' *The voice was calm and measured. I recognised it. It belonged to the shadow man. It belonged to the colour thief. He was calm because he had me in his complete control now. I tried to fight back with all the energy that I had left, with all the redness that still coursed through my body. I thrust my arms and legs out, and for a moment my hand connected with something and I half-managed to push myself up. But no... it was no use.*

'*Let go!*' *said the colour thief, and he loomed large, long fingers ready to snatch the last of my colour. He pressed the glass mask hard on my face and I felt my body grow weak. The world flickered like a faulty lightbulb and then everything went dark.*

6.03 a.m.

A whimper. I shot upright in bed. For a second, I thought the sound had come from me, but then Milo leaped from under my elbow and settled himself on the floor. I sensed that it had happened, even before I saw the mural. On it, a painted Milo stared back at his real life counterpart. His little black body was still leaping up at the younger version of me, but the red collar that I'd got him especially, with his name and our address on it, was no longer visible.

It was just a nightmare – a nightmare that kept coming back, but still just a nightmare. And I remained the only person who could see what the colour thief had stolen, which simply meant that it wasn't real.

A vague salty smell reached me from downstairs and I forced myself to get up, relieved it was staff training day and there was no school.

'Good morning,' said Aunty Lyn. When she smiled at me, her mouth looked like it was being held up on either side by tiny, invisible strings, and the lines around her eyes were deeper than normal.

'Good morning. I'm sorry about yesterday. I didn't mean what I said.'

'It's OK, Izzy. It's OK.' Her fingers combed through my hair, reminding me of Mum. She pointed to the table and pushed a bacon sandwich in my direction.

As I ate, she sat opposite me with a cup of coffee.

'Your dad's gone to see Dr Liz again,' she said, as if guessing the next question I was going to ask. 'She's got "doctor" in her title, but she's not a doctor of the sort that you would imagine. She's a counsellor and she helps people with the way that they're feeling. If it all goes well, he'll go and see her every week. I'm feeling confident that she'll help get him back on track. We won't worry as much then, will we?'

I wasn't sure what to say, but she looked positive, so I nodded.

'You know, Izzy, if you felt you ever wanted to talk to someone, I hope you'd let me or Dad know...?'

I nodded again. She was trying to understand and to help, but she didn't know... she hadn't been there.

'Can I go to Toby's?'

'Yes, of course. He seems like a lovely boy. He helped a lot in searching for you. He clearly cares a lot about you. Lots of people care about you being all right. Mona called for you last night – I almost forgot to tell you. She apologised for what she said in the science lab. I didn't ask her for details, but whatever it was, she said that she didn't mean it. Sometimes... sometimes people react badly to things that they don't understand.'

'I know.' I didn't need her to tell me that.

I finished my breakfast and slipped through the front door before she had a chance to say anything else.

When I saw Toby and Anna's house, I felt instantly better.

Toby was busy washing up and Anna was running around, ironing a white shirt and trying to find a pair of earrings.

'Mum's got her interview today. She's going for restaurant manager – the permanent position. It's D-Day. If she gets this, then we can stay here for sure.'

'Don't say it like that,' Anna wailed. 'I feel unprepared and I don't think I'll get it.'

I noticed that her usual spiky hair was smoothed over her ears and she was wearing more make-up than usual.

'Why not? You're amazing. You'll definitely get it.'

'These earrings or these?' Anna asked me.

'The pearl drops,' I told her. They made her look more professional.

She winked at me, ruffled Toby's hair and left the house in a hurry.

I got myself a glass of water and sat at the table, waiting for Toby to finish.

'Hey, I never showed you the house!' he said, pulling me into the living room, his hands still dripping with water.

'What do you mean? You've shown me round before.'

'No. No. I don't mean this house. I mean Spike's

house.' With everything that had happened, I'd forgotten about it entirely.

I gasped out loud when I saw it. I couldn't believe what an amazing job he'd done. The house had its own little roof complete with tin tiles to keep the rain out. It had three walls made of carefully sanded wood and even a veranda with two egg cups stuck to its floor at one end.

'One for grain and the other for water,' Toby explained, but of course I'd guessed that already.

'It just needs varnishing so that it doesn't rot and then I'll nail it to those two logs you so expertly tested,' he said. 'Then we can go and wedge it in the bush and it should be ready.'

We spent ages varnishing every bit of exposed wood, before Toby decided that the tin roof looked too dull and boring for Spike, and he would paint it red so that he would always be able to see his home from a distance.

'Look. That will be perfect! Mum used it to paint our front door,' he said, waving a tin at me.

His eyes narrowed. There was some element that he still wasn't happy with.

'You think something's missing?' I guessed, looking at the house from all angles. I wondered if he'd lost the plot and would want to build tiny bird furniture for Spike next.

I was surprised when he said: 'Could you give me a hand?'

It was an ordinary enough thing to ask, and he'd said it smiling at me in his usual, mysterious way. But at the same time, it was hugely important, because it was the first time he'd properly asked me to help. I remembered the moments when he'd sped away from me in his wheelchair before I managed to grab the handles, or when he'd dragged himself out of the water or up the stairs, just to prove he could.

'Would you be able to bring me a box from upstairs? It's a big blue one on top of the cupboard in Mum's room. It's the first door on the right.'

I had to stand on a chair to get it down. It was heavier than I expected. I looked curiously at the contents, a mishmash of treasures - football trophies, swimming medals, coins from different countries, computer games and envelopes of various shapes and sizes.

'What's all this stuff?'

'It's the Before Box.'

'The what?'

'The box of everything I had before the accident.'

I didn't know what to say to that, so I put it in his lap and went to the kitchen to get us a drink. I wasn't sure whether he would want me looking.

'I just wanted these.' He held up a plastic bag

with something inside. It was only when he emptied the contents that I saw that they were feathers of all colours and sizes.

'I collected these with Mum on Winston Beach in Norfolk. My nan used to live there and we'd visit her every summer. We had this tradition that we would always go on a really long run the first day we were there and collect lucky feathers on the way back. I saved the three most interesting ones each year.'

'They're great,' I said, picking up a few and arranging them into a fan. There was a long one in the middle that was white tinged with dark blue spots. I imagined how incredible the bird that it had come from would have been. An idea popped into my mind. Spike sometimes shed some of his feathers. They'd be grey but just as lucky. And there was someone I knew they could bring a bit of luck to. They'd be just right.

'What are you going to do with these?' I asked Toby.

'I'm going to line the house. Birds make nests out of twigs and feathers, and I thought we could help get him started. It'll make it softer and more comfortable.'

'Don't you want to keep them? You know, as a memento?'

'Nah,' he said, shaking his head.

When the house was ready, we took it back to mine to show Aunty Lyn and Dad, who had just come back from his meeting with Dr Liz.

'That swan had better be grateful,' he said. 'He's pretty much got a castle there.'

After lunch, they chatted about Project Elephant, which Toby genuinely loved and asked hundreds of questions about. He wanted to know how many elephants lived at the sanctuary in Kenya that Dad and Simon had helped to set up - there were fifty-four, which was a lot more than the last time I had asked. There had even been a couple of babies born in the past month.

'I would love to see them,' said Toby dreamily.

'I don't see why you couldn't,' said Dad. 'We aim to visit at least twice a year. We would just need to find a good time for you both to come.'

Toby was so distracted with everything Dad was showing him that by the time we actually made it to the river with an impatient Milo, it was late afternoon.

'Right,' he announced in the voice of an army general leading a battle, 'I trust you on this one, but I've got my camera at the ready just in case you do a repeat of last time.'

'Not if I do *this*!' I shouted triumphantly. I pulled his glasses off and ran down the bank, his protests ringing in my ears. It only took a minute to wedge the house neatly in the mulberry bush, although the river was high and I had to wade some of the way in. When I was happy that it was perfectly positioned, I went back to Toby and returned his vision to him.

Instantly he inspected my handiwork.

'Look! There!'

'What?'

It couldn't have been more perfectly timed. Spike appeared out of nowhere, swimming in our direction, as if he didn't have a care in the world. He seemed somehow more solid than before. He'd grown, and his feathers were less fluffy. He flexed his wings slightly, reminding me that one day, of course, he would be able to fly. He no longer seemed as if he would be blown away in a single gust.

'I'm going to get the fishing rod,' Toby said. 'I left it in the van.'

I nodded, determined not to lose sight of Spike. Milo stood next to me, also staring at him, as if in admiration. But the dangers were not yet over for our little bird. The moment Toby came back, the rod awkwardly under his armpit, Spike's siblings sensed that there might be dinner in the vicinity.

Milo barked at them, agitated.

'Nothing here for you,' I told them. 'You can fight for your own food at any time. This is for someone who can't yet.'

Toby took a potato from his pocket and broke a bit off, hooking it on to the rod. He swung the line over the water, but annoyingly it went right past Spike and caught on a clump of water grass.

He tugged at it, but the line wouldn't give.

There was nothing else for it. The cold water lapped at my ankles as I hooked my toes into the slimy mud, careful not to slip. I moved towards the clump of grass, like a wary traveller exploring a swamp.

As I disentangled the hook, I saw I was within touching distance of Spike who'd stayed in the same spot. He looked up at me.

Then, despite my certainty that he would scarper, I took the slightly damp potato off the hook and put it in the palm of my hand.

'Here,' I whispered, moving it towards him. Out of the corner of my eye I could see the other cygnets, but they were stopped by a low growl from the riverbank. Milo had once again acted in Spike's defence and his siblings retreated as if they had come up against an invisible wall.

Spike twitched his head to the side. He hesitated. We faced each other, frozen in time. And then with a jerk of his beak, so sudden that I would have missed it if I hadn't been concentrating hard, he snatched the morsel from my hand and swallowed it whole.

He shuddered and automatically moved backwards, as if scared about what he'd done. I remained perfectly still. Moments later, he tried again. Soon, all the potato had gone. Toby sent more on the end of the rod when I had an idea. I motioned in the direction of the house where we'd already put food into one of the egg cups.

At first, Spike didn't figure out what was happening, but he edged closer and closer to the house, and I rewarded him each time he moved in the right direction.

And then, just as I felt that my chest would burst with anticipation, he made a leap on to the veranda of the little house and grabbed the food in the cup.

I turned to Toby, grinning as he raised his camera to take a photo.

'This is your home,' I told Spike. 'You'll have to fight the others off yourself next time, but this place might help. We won't be here.'

I sat down on the grass next to Toby, my bare feet freezing, but I felt happy. Milo was nestled in his favourite spot on his lap.

'You did it,' Toby whispered. 'I don't know how, but you did it.'

'We both did. You did more than me.'

He looked at me then and asked unexpectedly, 'Do you ever feel like doing a life swap with somebody, even if it's just for a day or an hour - just to know for that snippet of time what it's like to be them?'

I smiled, because although it had hardly been any time at all, he already knew me so well.

'I used to do it a lot. I used to watch actresses on TV and want to jump into their skin, just for that one take of a film. And you?'

'Oh, loads of people,' he said, and he got that hazy look in his eyes when I really couldn't tell what he was thinking. 'Just now I was imagining what it would be like to be Spike.'

'Scary, I reckon.'

'Oh, yeah, the world must seem super-scary, but don't you think it's exciting too? He's been through a lot of change, and now he has so many amazing possibilities before him. He can go anywhere he wants.'

'Of course,' I said. And thinking about it that way made me realise that a little bit of what Toby was saying was true of me too. It was almost as if Spike and I had been helping one another.

Just as we were leaving, I noticed the feathers clustered in the branches of Spike's bush. I carefully pulled a few of the prettiest ones out and put them in my pocket. I was surprised to find that in my hand they seemed strong and sturdy, despite the small bits of fluff that still remained at the edges. His wings would soon be able to carry his weight and he would be ready to fly.

I kept one feather for myself and the other for somebody who I knew could use a bit of Spike's strength.

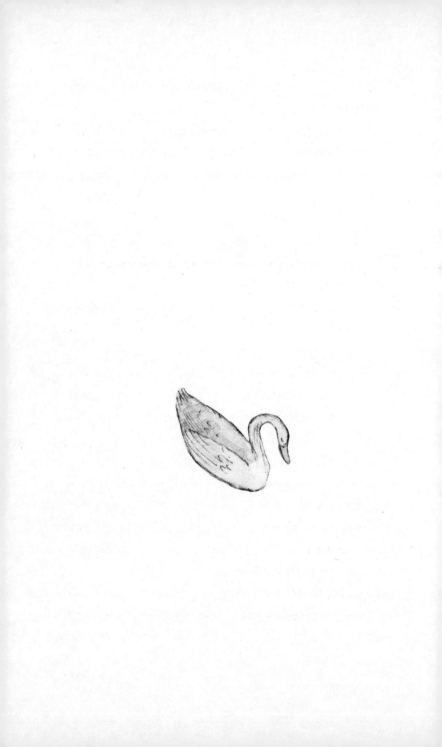

Sixteen

Back at Toby's house, he showed me the research he had put together after he'd found Spike.

'It has all the facts in there. The ones I used to test you on.'

'Of course. It's how you became the swan geek.'

It seemed a lifetime ago that I'd first seen Spike's tufty little head. He looked nothing like that old version of himself now. He was stronger and more graceful, and his fluff was beginning to disappear.

I sat at the kitchen table, reading through the rest of the booklet. Toby had kept everything - there were sketches of the wooden house and the fishing rod mechanism and plenty of photos: of Spike, of me and Milo at the water's edge looking for Spike, and of Spike's fantastic, newly painted house.

Toby looked at me from across the table and said, 'It's your turn to tell me - remember you said you would?'

We both knew exactly what he was talking about. The pit of my stomach turned cold, but then he smiled and something in me changed.

The words came spilling out. I started at the beginning. I told him about the nightmare, the shadow man and the colour thief and the daily disappearance of a new colour, visible only to me.

He listened, his forehead creased with concentration. And the more I spoke, the more rapid my story became. A river of words gushed from my mouth.

I was certain he wouldn't believe me. He'd explode into laughter at any moment. But he didn't, and I continued.

'... and last night. Last night I dreamed that he'd finally won. I was fighting him but I had no energy left. He was just shouting for me to let go. And when I woke up and looked at my wall, I saw that Milo's collar was no longer red, and I knew that it was true.'

'And you haven't told anyone? Why?'

'I didn't think anyone would believe me. My dad didn't notice a thing when he came and looked at the mural. It's in my head, Toby. It's only in my own stupid head.'

I was surprised at how calm I sounded when inside I felt as if something was trying to break out of my chest.

'But couldn't you have told your dad? Your aunt?'

'They have bigger things to worry about,' I said.

'Izzy, this *is* big,' he told me. 'It's as big as you get. It's *huge*.'

'You're not going to tell them, are you?' I could imagine the look on Aunty Lyn's face - a combination of impatience, confusion and worry. There would be nothing that she could do, of course. There was nothing anyone could do.

'No, of course not. Not if you don't want me to. But I'm going to think about how to help you. We can't leave you like this.'

He held out his hand to pull me to my feet.

She came to me in a dream that night for the first time. There were no tubes and no beeping heart monitor. She stood in my room, her eyes narrowed in a look of concentration, sketching the outline of the next scene on the mural. I wanted to reach out and touch her, but somehow she was too far away.

She was wearing her favourite light-blue dungarees and her hair was swept up in a messy ponytail that was specked with paint. Milo ran round her feet, knocking over pots, spilling paint on to the sheet that had been carefully laid on the floor. She shooed him away, but only half-heartedly. She didn't mind him there, not really.

'Colour me in!' I said. She picked up a paintbrush, dipped it in the pot of yellow, and brushed the tip of my nose.

'You know I will. As soon as I've finished this.'

I was trying to hold still so that she could draw my profile, but my head kept drooping from tiredness. If only I could stay awake, if only I could fight the urge to sleep, then maybe she would...

'Izzy! Izzy!' The urgent call echoed through the silence of the night, followed by a rattle on glass. My dazed brain took a while to register that the sound was real. I didn't want to leave the dream... I wasn't ready.

But the shouting didn't stop. I sat up in bed, rubbing my eyes, and realised that it was coming from the outside. I dragged myself from under the covers. The numbers on the alarm clock glowed – 4.26 a.m.

In the light of the street lamp Toby gazed up at me from the garden. He was holding a handful of pebbles. With his other hand, he beckoned me to come down.

I quickly put a jumper over my pyjama top. I padded downstairs careful not to wake Aunty Lyn, reassured by the steady snoring coming from Dad's room. Milo didn't stir from his usual spot. I thrust my bare feet into a pair of trainers. My fingers fumbled for a set of keys in the bowl by the front door and found them. I crept out into the night.

Toby put a finger to his lips and I followed him, his wheels creaking quietly, as we made our way to the gate.

It was like walking in a dream. The street around me blurred and swayed. Toby's wheels gleamed in the dark, as his hands pushed in a steady rhythm.

It was only when we were safely in the alleyway that led to the river that he whispered: 'I think I've figured it out, Izzy!'

'What?'

'I've been thinking all night. I couldn't sleep. The colour thief was shouting at you to let go, wasn't he?'

'Yeah...'

'Did he say what he wanted you to let go of?'

'From whatever I was holding on to. I don't know.'

'That's the thing,' said Toby triumphantly. 'You've been holding on to it, holding on to that terrible day.'

'I don't understand,' I said. I was shivering now. Toby was partly obscured by the garage of the house next door, his face cut in half by a wedge of silvery light.

'You have to release it. You've been holding it inside all this time. Now you must let it go.'

'I can't do it, Toby.' I wanted to crawl back into the safe warmth of my bed, but my body was rigid, frozen.

'You can,' he insisted. 'I know you can.'

149

It began to rain. The drizzle cooled my burning face.

'Please.' He squeezed my hand and pulled me gently in the direction of the river. 'Please try. Let's go inside the van.'

The blackness was all-consuming. It was impossible to make out where the mud ended and the river began.

'I should have brought a torch,' said Toby. 'I left the house so quickly that I forgot.'

We moved slowly through the darkness, careful not to steer in the direction of the water. I held on to the handles of Toby's wheelchair, more to steady myself than him. Through the regular smack of Toby's palms on his wheels I heard the flutter of wings, which made me think of Spike's feathers. I knew that somewhere in the depths of the night, his mum was protecting her offspring from any unexpected intruders. I felt reassured by her presence.

'Toby, let's come back another time,' I whispered, 'I can't do it now. I don't want to...'

But he had already wheeled himself all the way to the back of the van and motioned for me to give him a hand getting out of his wheelchair.

We made it just at the moment when the clouds opened and the rain began to pelt down in solid sheets. We sat leaning against opposite sides of the van, our feet touching.

'Don't you love the night?' he whispered. 'Things look different somehow, more real than by day. You get the sense that some of the most important things happen when the rest of the world is sleeping.'

It was true. There was something magical about the night. Time swung suspended at night; it didn't leak away at its normal speed. The van was filled with a restful peace.

But the knowledge of what I was about to do made the spiders wild. They had woken up and were now crawling through my insides, higher and higher towards the tiny compartment in my mind; the storage box of memory which housed *that* day.

'It will be the most awful thing, but you have to do it,' Toby said, guessing my thoughts. 'I did it, Izzy, and I think I'm far more of a chicken than you.'

'Stop it,' I began. I knew what I wanted to say to him. It was there inside my head, ready to come out. I wanted to say that he was the bravest person I knew - that he was incredible at coping in a world that wasn't designed for people like him, that he was the first person who had understood what I felt... But I surprised myself by beginning a very different sentence.

'It was the last day of school before the summer holidays. We were doing up the bedrooms and the whole house smelled of paint. I wanted my room to be a bright yellow, because it would remind me of summer all year round, and I came home from school that day to find Mum with yellow paint splattered everywhere. She insisted on doing all of the decorating herself and she did more than just paint the walls. She was a real artist, and before I was even born she'd had the great idea of making a mural in my room, showing important events in my life.

'"We can add to it as you grow up," she'd said, when I was old enough to understand. The first picture was of all of us in hospital on the day I was born. I was a huge baby, the biggest on the ward, and I was born with lots of hair. Mum had painted the three of us, taking lots of care with every brush stroke so it ended up looking so realistic. You can even see the nurses in the background and some of the other bawling babies on the ward.

'The next picture was of me as a three-year-old, when I'd decided to cut off my own hair. I'm sitting on the grass with these funny tufts sticking up all over my head.'

'Like Spike?' Toby asked.

'I suppose so, yes. Then there was me with a giant backpack on my first day of school and so on, until... that day.

'She wanted me to pose, but I was in a rush. She was supposed to be taking me to a concert, picking Lou up on the way, and I had to get changed quickly and take all my stuff. And I was angry with Mum because she didn't have dinner ready and she hadn't ironed my only good blue dress. And then she was talking for ages on the phone to Mr Leah - they share an art studio. I wanted...'

'You wanted?'

'I wanted for her to be more like Lou's mum. She always spent lots of money on Lou and took us both to great places - films, theme parks, shopping. And my mum... was scatty and disorganised. She worked as a teaching assistant to kids with special needs and she wore baggy jumpers and jeans. And that day, she hadn't made dinner and decided that we would just have egg and chips.

'And she went to the kitchen and whipped out this silly mould for making fried eggs in the shape of an elephant, thinking it would make me laugh. One of the kids from school had given it to her. But I had no time for it because I had nothing to wear and I was annoyed at her. By the time I'd got ready and we'd eaten, we were running really late.'

I could barely recognise my own shaking voice in the silence of the van.

'What happened?'

'We got into her car. It used to belong to my grandpa

and I loved it. It had brown seats which still smelled of leather and were deep and bouncy. Dad used to always say proudly that the car was a proper classic. It made me feel like a lady being driven back to her manor house in the country. But that day I was just scared that I was going to miss the concert.

'I kept asking Mum to take shortcuts and go faster, and she took a quicker route, past the petrol station. We were really nearly on Lou's road. I was putting on my lipgloss in the mirror and out of the corner of my eye, I could see a purple car racing down the road that crossed with ours. I was certain that Mum had seen it too, but she hadn't. The lights were flashing orange – they hadn't changed to green. Mum saw the car in the lane next to hers starting up so she hit the accelerator.'

I breathed out – I realised suddenly how much speed I'd gathered as I spoke. My mouth was parched but I couldn't stop now that I'd got this far.

'Next thing I saw a flash of purple to my right and felt a massive thump. It all happened in seconds. I turned and I saw Mum's face, filled with hopeless, horrible panic. Then everything was black.'

Seventeen

'But that day didn't end with everything turning black?' asked Toby.

'No, no, it didn't... although I really, really wished that it had done. I only fainted for a minute at most, and when I came round, I was still sitting in the same position. For a moment everything was scarily quiet and then suddenly the sounds came flooding in - police and ambulance sirens, people shouting, cars slowing down. There was smoke everywhere and flashing lights and this horrible smell of petrol and rubber that made me want to gag.

'I knew that something was very wrong, but I hesitated and then I turned my head to the right. And she was there, her head resting on the steering wheel, her hair spread out all over. Her left arm was pale and freckly with little smudges of yellow paint.

'But to her right, there was no longer a door and everything that was left was red. There was so much red and it seemed to expand at such an awful rate that I couldn't look any more.

'I sat and stared at a tiny smudge of yellow on the soft inside of her left elbow. I think I was semi-conscious, but that's when the shadow man came and tried to get me, but I didn't want to leave Mum. My limbs felt like lead. I couldn't stop him shouting, couldn't stop the red, and I just couldn't help her – I couldn't help my mum.'

'You went to hospital?' asked Toby.

'Yes, although there was nothing wrong with me apart from the back of my neck, which felt really sore. They said I was on the "good side". I suppose they meant the side that the purple car didn't hit.

'Mum was on the bad side. They said that it was such a huge force and over so quickly that she wouldn't have felt any pain.

'Next time I saw her, she wasn't covered in red any more and the look of panic was gone. She was there, lying white and peaceful. She had an awful head injury and the doctors had put her into a coma, but her heart was still beating.

'They said they needed to wait for the swelling in her brain to go down and that they didn't know when... that they didn't know *if* she would be OK again. And it's my fault. It's all my fault. I just sat there stupidly and held her hand... but I couldn't cry. It felt worse than the worst feeling in the world and I couldn't cry.'

'Until now...' said Toby.

He was right. For the very first time since it happened, oceans of tears were spilling from my eyes, sliding down the side of my nose. They were coming so fast that I could barely brush them away with my hand. My vision went hazy, my nose was running and my body heaved. I sobbed and sobbed, for Mum lying there so helplessly, for Dad and his tired eyes, for Aunty Lyn, for Toby and his box of treasures, for the world as it was before, for every single one of the colours that had disappeared. And then I allowed myself, just a little, to cry for me.

'Why now?' Toby asked.

'I... I don't know.'

'Because you've let go. Nobody knew the whole of it until now and you didn't dare tell anyone.'

'Because it was my fault.'

'It wasn't your fault.'

'It was. If I hadn't made her drive me to that stupid, awful concert, it wouldn't have happened. I was the one who made her rush... who told her off on that last day for not ironing my dress! For not making dinner on time!'

'You didn't make her crash, Izzy. You didn't tell her to go when it was dangerous.'

'But she wouldn't have been there if it wasn't for me!'

'Of course,' he said. 'Everything is linked to everything else. You wouldn't be sitting here with me now if it wasn't for your mum. But it doesn't mean it was your fault, Izzy. I might not have been on the roof of that garage if it wasn't for Chai, but I didn't ever think that the accident was *his* fault.'

'You didn't?'

'No. And you thinking you're to blame is just that - you thinking. It's not what happened. You have your own version of the Blackest Day... Anyway, when was it that the colour thief first arrived in your nightmare? What happened on that day?'

I thought about it hard.

'My best friend from school, Lou, was acting weird towards me,' I began, and then I realised that wasn't true. That had been the day *after* the nightmare. The day before, I had been to the hospital to see Mum for the first time since the accident. I didn't even get as far as the room - I only looked through the glass. Now that I thought back, I remembered that it was the first time that I properly allowed myself to understand that she might never come home and I'd known that it was because of what *I* had done. By not visiting her earlier, I hadn't had to face that thought.

'You weren't there, Toby... I could have done something! I could have reacted quicker!'

'I know I wasn't there. Nobody was, apart from you and your mum. That doesn't mean...'

But I didn't hear the end of that sentence, because something suddenly dawned on me. Toby was wrong - there *had* been another person, another person who'd witnessed it, who'd seen exactly what had happened. Shelley.

As the morning light began to spread through the sky, I knew what I had to do.

'Come on,' I said to Toby. 'I'd like you to come with me to visit someone.'

It was Lou's dad who opened the door in his pyjamas, looking anxious.

'What's going on? Oh, it's you, Izzy. Has something happened? Are you all right?'

'Yes, yes,' I said impatiently. 'Is Shelley in?'

'Yes, of course. I'll get her. Is everything OK with Lou?'

'What? Isn't she at home?' In the swift march to their house, I hadn't even considered what would happen if I came face to face with Lou.

'She's gone to some sleepover.'

Luckily, at that point, Shelley appeared behind him.

'Izzy, what are you doing here? What's the time?' she asked bewildered.

'Just coming up to six-thirty a.m.,' Toby informed her, looking at his watch. I'd had no idea how early it was. I felt embarrassed for having come at such a ridiculous hour. But now that I was here, it would be worse to suddenly leave.

'I... I wanted to ask you something,' I told her. 'Would it be all right if I came in? And... this is my friend Toby. Could he come in too?'

The three of us sat around the kitchen table, our hands wrapped around mugs of steaming tea. Lou's dad had disappeared upstairs after he'd been assured that his daughter was perfectly safe and had nothing to do with my early morning arrival. It was strange being back here. Nothing had changed. Even the stain on the blind from the chocolate sauce bottle that had exploded in Lou's hands was still there. That was from when we'd made chocolate cakes for New Year's Eve. It seemed a lifetime ago.

'Nice to meet you,' Shelley said to Toby. 'Are you in Lou and Izzy's class?'

'Not yet, but I hope maybe I will be next year.'

'Right... so why is it that you're here?'

'It's about the accident,' I said to her, staring at the gingham tablecloth. 'I want to know what happened.'

Shelley was quiet for a moment.

'Which part, Izzy? Surely you know...'

'Could you tell me what you saw?'

'Of course I can, but I don't see how that would help...' she started. 'It will be a horrible thing for you to hear, Izzy, and I don't...'

'It would help,' Toby told her. 'It really would.'

'Why?'

'Because—'

'No, don't say anything,' I said to him pleadingly. 'Let Shelley tell it.'

She closed her eyes and I assumed that it was in protest against reliving those awful moments. Minutes passed in silence, each one making me wonder whether this had been a terrible idea. My chair scraped on the kitchen floor and Shelley's eyelids flickered open.

'I'll tell you,' she said and motioned for me to sit back down.

'Your mum rang to say that you were running late, but she said that she could drive you all the way to the venue to save me the journey. I had to check in on Lou's grandma that day, as she'd been taken to hospital. So Lou stayed in the house to wait for you and I set off into town. I'd reached the end of the road when I saw

161

it happen. You'd just left the junction with the traffic lights and a purple car came speeding from the right. It all happened in an instant.'

'Had the lights changed?'

'Sorry?'

'Had Mum jumped the lights?'

'What? No, of course she hadn't.'

I stared at her, desperately trying to see whether she was lying, trying to protect me from the truth.

'I don't remember seeing them turn green,' I told her.

'Oh, Izzy, how would you be expected to remember such a thing?'

'But you don't have any proof that I didn't make Mum jump the lights?'

'Proof? How do you mean? You weren't the first car at the lights, Izzy. There was another in front of you. I remember that distinctly because the one directly in front was a red Mini that narrowly avoided the hit. So that's proof that you couldn't have jumped the lights. The Mini driver was in shock, but not in as much shock as I was. He was the one who rang the ambulance and the fire brigade. I couldn't do it.'

It was only when I noticed the tiny splashes on the edge of the table that I realised that I was crying again. Tears of relief came flooding from somewhere deep inside me, somewhere deeper than I had ever explored. Shelley leaned over and hugged me close.

'Carry on. Please carry on,' I begged her.

'There isn't much else to say, Izzy,' she told me. 'The car was smoking by then and it was so hot that I didn't dare come any closer. The paramedics arrived quickly. They had some trouble getting you out. One of them had to cut through the seatbelt and lift you...'

'Green - he was wearing green.'

'Was he? Yes, they have dark green uniforms, don't they? He was a nice young chap. He got you on to a stretcher and put an oxygen mask...'

'The colour thief!' I interrupted her. 'He's the colour thief!'

'Sorry?'

And that was when all of the scattered images from my nightmares rearranged themselves into a train of events I could finally understand. This man had arrived to pull me out of the smoking car and tried his best to stop me from seeing what had happened to Mum, who, of course, was on my right-hand side. 'Don't look right!' he'd repeated over and over. He must have struggled to free me, and by the time he'd succeeded, I would've breathed in a lot of smoke. That was where the oxygen mask had come in and then he would have strapped me to a stretcher and lifted me into an ambulance.

'It was a paramedic all along,' Toby whispered in disbelief. 'He was trying to help you, to get you to safety.'

'I know... and I thought that he was doing the opposite - that he was trying to hurt me, and that he was stealing the colours...'

'Are you all right, Izzy?' asked Shelley, not following a word we were saying.

'I'm good,' I whispered to her. 'Thank you. Thank you *so much*.'

Eighteen

'You look different,' said Frank.

'Do I? How?' I'd enjoyed the walk to school that day for the first time in weeks. I'd walked slowly, taking in the clear blue sky, the yellow, red and orange of the last fallen leaves. They mirrored the colours on the mural, which had returned, of course. When we came home from seeing Shelley, I ran up to my bedroom to check and there they were - looking exactly as they had done before the arrival of the colour thief, who I now knew had never really been a colour thief at all.

'Not sure,' he said. 'Just different. In a good way.' He blushed a deep shade of crimson and ducked his head under the desk, pretending that he was picking something up off the floor. Cormack Griffiths and his mates would've had a field day if they'd seen Frank now.

When he re-emerged he said, 'It's up, you know. It's official.'

'What is?'

'The cast list on the staffroom door. The big news, of course, is that I'm chief lighting technician. I'll sit in the box at the back of the hall – you know the one with the flashing buttons. I get to move the big spotlights around, maybe even drop them on the heads of people that I don't like. If you have any requests, send them my way.'

I rolled my eyes.

'I was joking. I mean I *am* chief technician, but that's not the big news. The big news is that you're Lady Macbeth.'

'What? Seriously?' I felt like giving him a hug.

'Yep.'

I couldn't believe that Mr Winch had decided to give it to me after everything that had happened.

It was an amazing start to the morning and the day improved when Harpreet came up to me at break and said, 'Sorry about the other day. I was stupid and I didn't know what I was saying. I don't think you're dangerous. You just got mad, that's all, and you had a right to. Is that what made you run off? What we said?' she asked, looking at the floor.

'It was only a small part. Don't worry about it,' I told her.

Others had now clearly seen the cast list because a few of them came over to congratulate me, including

Mona, who'd been given the role of Lady Macduff.

Jemima was cast as the messenger and Lou was assigned to the team building the set.

I could see her scowling in the corner of the classroom, but I no longer cared.

In art, Mr Leah congratulated me too.

'I saw the great news,' he said, coming over as we were finishing our project on the interpretation of dreams. Today, the dark figure in my painting looked far less menacing.

'Your mum would be proud,' Mr Leah said. 'I'm sure she would have wanted to commemorate it in some way.'

His words sparked an idea in my head.

'Is it all right if I borrow some paints?' I asked him.

'Yes, of course. You know where they live,' he said, sweeping his hand across to the cupboards.

'Thank you.'

'And, Izzy?'

'Yes.'

'It's good to see you smile.'

That day I ran home with my bag filled with tubs of acrylic paint, which I emptied out in a heap on my bedroom floor. The first thing I did was to use the white and yellow to soften the edges of the dark ragged storm that I'd created when I'd painted the Blackest Day.

Then, in the clear space on the other side of it, I began to paint the next scene.

I drew the outline of the riverbank surrounded by seeping brown mud. Then the emerald-green of the river plants and the smudge of Milo running around on the bank. Next came the outline of Toby, busily hooking scraps on to the end of his fishing rod. His glasses had, as always, fallen down his nose. I was beside him, sitting with my trousers rolled up and my feet bare, ready to wade into the water to feed Spike, who was perched on the veranda of his new home, his feathers ruffled against the wind.

Next to this picture, I had left a special place that could be painted in time.

I surveyed my work of art. It wasn't even close to Mum's standards, but I think she would have liked it nonetheless.

I was adding the finishing touches to Spike's wings when the doorbell rang.

Toby sat outside with an enormous grin on his face.

'She got the job!' he shouted when he saw me. 'She got the job!'

'That's incredible! Does that mean that you're definitely staying?'

'Yep. Mum's decided that she'll use some of her first month's salary on renovation. We'll start by doing her bedroom and then mine. I've already volunteered you to help. I hope that's OK.'

'I'd love to!'

But first, of course, we went to the river, to check in on our favourite feathered friend.

'I saw him this morning,' said Toby. Then he suddenly clamped his mouth shut, as if remembering that he wasn't supposed to tell me anything.

The weekend had brought with it a sudden cold spell, and a lot of the mud beneath us had turned to ice.

I scanned the water. There was no sign of the swans.

'Look, there,' said Toby impatiently, pointing in the direction of Spike's house. I crept closer and watched and within moments, I burst out laughing.

Because there was Spike, sitting in his house, stuffing his beak with something delicious. Two of his siblings were trying to force their way into his home to steal his food, but our hero was having none of it. He fought them off with his wings, and after a short scuffle, to my amazement, they backed away.

'Where did he get that from?' I asked Toby, trying and failing to make out what Spike was eating.

'I don't know.' Toby shrugged. 'I didn't give it to him and the mother swan is nowhere in sight. Which can only mean one thing - that he managed to get it for himself.'

'Spike, you did it!' '

'Absolutely. We've got proof now.'

'He's going to be all right, isn't he?'

'Of course. I told you, didn't I? All he needed was a bit of help.'

Macbeth was on in the last week of school before Christmas. Milton High School had always been unusual when it came to theatre. Other schools had Christmas plays and carol concerts, whereas we had Shakespeare. I was glad we did. The month in the run-up to the production was filled with rehearsals. They were on almost every day after school and I had to be in almost every single one of them.

I spent any free time helping Toby with his room. Anna and I took apart Toby's clunky old bed and replaced it with a new one, which was smaller and easier for him to get in and out of. Then we dismantled the old boiler cupboard and put in a new desk which Toby could use for everything from schoolwork to building things.

When I was leaving I noticed a box lying among the pile of things at the end of the corridor, ready to be put into Toby's room. There were a couple of paintbrushes in it, a menu from Anna's new restaurant, *Balti Towers*, slats of wood from the building of Spike's house and the photo that Toby took of me feeding Spike on the veranda.

The Box of After, it said on the side.

And, of course, I visited Mum. She still lay in the same bed, a shadow of her old self. The doctor had told Dad a few days earlier that the swelling in her head had gone down, though, which was a good sign. There was no day set yet for bringing her out of the coma, but there was real hope that it would happen.

The sight of her room no longer frightened me. I barely heard the beeps of the machine.

I'd taken her Spike's feather a while back. I'd twirled it in between her fingers so she could feel how it was strong and soft at the same time, and then I'd popped it in a tiny vase on her bedside table.

'People might think that you're weak,' I'd said aloud. 'Or that you're not going to make it... but then it turns out that you're stronger than you think. And sometimes you just need a bit of help. I brought you this from Spike, who proves it's true. I think you two would really like each other.'

And as I talked, an image formed in my head of going down to the riverbank with Mum to introduce her to Spike. We would get there just as he was spreading his wings, wings which by now would be almost completely white. Maybe he would fly just a short distance to begin with, as nothing ever seems easy the first time you do it, but then he would try again and again and each time he would fly a little higher.

Today I told Mum about how excited and scared I was about playing Lady Macbeth and I gripped her hand tightly, in the way that I would normally do before going on stage. And even though she couldn't squeeze back, I could almost hear her saying, as she always did, 'You're going to whizz them away. You'd better watch out that you don't lose your hearing from all the clapping.' And deep down I knew she was right - I didn't have to be scared. Of anything.

Nineteen

It was the opening night of the play. I was waiting behind the curtain with Frank, who was backstage, when he should have been in the lighting box.

'Bet you're petrified,' he said.

'Frank, shut up.'

'I'm only saying it because I know that you'll be awesome.'

'I haven't rehearsed enough. What if I forget where to go, or even worse, what if I forget my lines?'

'You're fine. Remember to repeat "out" twice in "out, out damned spot". That's the only thing you got wrong on Friday. Other than that you memorised everything.'

Frank had stayed after school every night the previous week, directing me to where I should be standing in each scene and testing me on my lines. There is no way I would've learned them in time without his help.

'Go on, you're up, you're up!' he said now, and motioned for me to step forward.

It all happened so quickly. Just two steps and suddenly the lights illuminated me and I'd no doubt that I could do this. I no longer felt bland and grey - I felt coloured in, in full technicolour and I wanted to do this for Mum. Even the tightness of the corset of my dress, or the beads of sweat on my forehead didn't matter, because the words came out as they were always meant to. I moved around the stage with ease, and remembered every single word. There was one thing that was different, though. I could still imagine Lady Macbeth's guilt - it was a feeling I'd known so well for so long, but I knew now that I was nothing like her. She had deliberately gone out to hurt people, and that wasn't me at all.

I was half-aware of the cheering by the end of the scene, but it wasn't over yet. It was only with the final curtain call that I allowed myself to breathe properly and to look out at the audience. I was searching for some very important spectators. My eyes scanned the rows of chairs. And there they were - at the front, right behind the Sergeant, who caught my eye and gave me a thumbs-up. She looked far less frightening in her casual clothes, without her 'army uniform'. Toby was whistling and clapping like mad. Next to him Anna, Aunty Lyn and Uncle Tom beamed with pride.

And on the other side of Toby, Dad was on his feet, giving me a standing ovation. He looked at me, our eyes locked and he winked.

He was waiting for me at the door of the Green Room after the play, where Mona and Harpreet were helping me out of my corset.

'You were even more specsational than I expected,' he said, and I saw real laughter in his eyes. 'Even Lou said so.'

'Lou came to see it?'

'Yes, she was sitting just a few rows behind us with her mum. And did you see that Simon came too, with his wife? He said you were the best Lady Macbeth he'd ever seen.'

Dad had been back at work for a week now and things were going well. Project Elephant was already preparing for a trip to Kenya in the spring to visit a new elephant sanctuary to see how it could be supported.

Dad whispered in my ear, 'You know she's always incredibly proud of you, don't you? She would have loved this.'

My heart sped up for a moment then, but I squeezed his hand and nodded because I knew it was true. And she'd been right about the clapping - it had been the loudest that I'd ever had. I would go back again tomorrow to tell Mum about how everything went and I knew, somehow, I knew she would be well again. She just needed a little bit of help.

As we left, I found myself in a crowd of classmates all wanting to congratulate me, among them Mr Winch, who shook my hand and told me, 'I've already got a great role in mind for you for next year's show!'

Then Aunty Lyn came over and gave me a hug.

'I can't put into words how good you were,' she told me. She brushed her hand against her left eye causing a mascara smudge. 'I'm going to miss you.'

'What do you mean?'

'Well, I think you and your dad are going to do all right without me. You will. And you know I'm always at the end of the phone if you need me. I'll come straightaway, anytime.'

'Yes, I know. Thanks for staying with us,' I said. 'It made a big difference.' I smiled at her, because I realised how true it was.

'I'm glad to hear you say that. And you know what? I'm going to see you in a couple of weeks anyway, because we'll all descend on you for Christmas.'

'You're coming here? That's great.'

'Yes, if you don't mind. I thought about inviting Anna and Toby too, because Anna mentioned that they wouldn't be going back north, as they'd originally planned.'

I hadn't dared think about Christmas. I knew, of course, that it was coming in the not too distant future, but I just couldn't imagine it with Mum still in hospital. It had always been the four of us – me, Mum, Dad and Milo.

Toby was waiting for me in the corner of the car park, Milo asleep on his lap.

'I'd better get used to this place,' he said. 'I'll be spending a lot of time here next term.'

'You got accepted?' I felt as if there were fireworks going off in my stomach. I couldn't believe that he'd waited this long to tell me.

'Yep. Your school passed all the tests for ramps and good wheelchair access so I'll be here from January.'

'No way!'

'Do you think they'll let us sit together?'

I was going to answer yes, but then I remembered that I had a very loyal desk companion already.

'Sure, although I currently sit next to Frank...'

'Ah, the one from the lighting box?'

'You know him?'

'We talked a bit after the show. He seems all right. I'm only kidding, you know – it doesn't matter where I sit. Everyone I've met so far seems great.'

'They are.'

And I meant it. There was the possible exception of Lou, but she strangely didn't bother me that much now. The old Lou belonged to the world before the Blackest

Day. Maybe she would return one day, but at the moment I was just fine without her.

I spent the next half an hour hugging and chatting to everyone who had come to see the play and I still felt a rush of victory as I skipped along next to Toby on the way home, just a bit ahead of Dad, Aunty Lyn and Anna.

Soon, the laughter and shouts grew distant and all I could hear was the sound of Toby's wheels turning on the pavement. I breathed in, savouring the smell of the cold December night. And I could have been imagining it but somewhere from the direction of the river, I thought I could hear the faint flutter of wings. I wondered if it was Spike, showing everyone who was boss. After all, my lucky feathers had come from those very wings.

Acknowledgements

A big thank you to my amazing editor Fiona Kennedy and the wonderful team at Head of Zeus, who brought this book to life. An equally big shout out to my patient and encouraging agent Kate Hordern who believed in it from the start, even when it needed a lot of work.

Thank you to my first readers, Giles, Deeps, Suzie, Poppy, Beth, Helena, Will and Francine, to my supportive and constructively critical creative writing group from Curtis Brown Creative, and to everyone who encouraged me to persevere with finally finishing the manuscript, especially my mum, Agata and Sophie.

A belated thank you also to my dad, who inspired my love of books from an early age. I hope he would have liked this one.

It's been a long but exciting journey.

Ewa Jozefkowicz
London
January 2018

Readers' Notes

Structure

Look at the title of the book: *The Mystery of the Colour Thief.*

Discuss: Think about the word 'mystery'. What is a mystery book?

Activity: You may wish to consider 'key elements' of the mystery genre.

These include:
- a sense of foreboding
- an unsolved crime
- clues
- a detective
- witnesses
- wrong turns or red herrings
- a cliffhanger moment or danger
- resolution

See if you can identify all these features in the book. Where do they appear? Highlight the passages or make a note of the page numbers.

Discuss: 'A colour thief'. What does this mean?

Can a person really steal colour? Or is it metaphorical? What is a metaphor?

Activity: Now think about what it would feel like if the world lacked certain colours. Draw a 'colour by numbers' scene with simple shapes, attributing 1 to green, 2 to red etc, but don't colour them in, just write the number inside each shape. Give to your classmate/ partner and have them colour in the scene according to your numbers. Do one colour at a time. Think about what the colours do to the scene. Do they make it fresher, more lively? Do they give it atmosphere? What about if you take the same scene, and colour it all shades of the same colour? Does it change the feel of the picture?

Now read the first chapter of the book.

Discuss: Why has the author chosen to start her book with a dream? Just from reading the first chapter, what do you think the dream means?

Activity: Write a diary entry from Izzy's point of view after reading Chapter One. Which emotions do you feel?

Once you have read the whole book, take a look at just the dream sequences. These are on the following pages 1, 35, 71, 97, 131.

Discuss: What clues do they give about the colour thief? What else can you piece together from reading the dream sequences as one?

The explanation to the dreams and the resolution of the mystery is revealed on page 163.

Discuss: Did you solve the mystery before then? Could the dream sequences mean anything else? Were there any red herrings?

One of Izzy's dreams is not in italics. See page 147.

Discuss: Why is this?

Activity: Write your own dream diary over a fortnight. Can you see patterns in your dreams? Do they give clues about your own life? Now share your dream diaries with your classmates. See if there are similarities.

According to scientists, there are certain dream symbols that we all share. Popular symbols include: being chased, falling, a test at school, flying, and food. Do any of these feature in your dreams? Make a list and write down what you think each one means.

Discuss: Do you think dreams tell us about the future, like Joseph's, or about events in the past, like Izzy's in *The Mystery of the Colour Thief*?

Characters

Ewa Jozefkowicz is very good at portraying people through the things they wear or have about them.

'Even the usual crowds of sixth formers with their slouchy rucksacks and rolled-up blazer sleeves had disappeared inside' (page 2).

'The two screens of her computer were placed at what looked like an exact forty-five degree angle from one another, and out of the corner of my eye, I caught the glimmer of a gold-nibbed fountain pen, lying in its special velvet green holder' (page 78).

Discuss: Think about what these two sentences tell you about the sixth formers and the headmistress?

Aunty Lyn is described on page 102: 'she was still in her pyjama bottoms and an oversized jumper, and without make-up her face looked different - softer.'

And Lou, on page 107, 'had a large white bandage stuck to the side of her head. Get Well Soon cards were arranged in an elaborate display in front of her.'

Discuss: Do clothes and accessories make people appear different from how they might be inside? Think about Aunty Lyn when Izzy first mentions her in Chapter Seven. Look at how Lou manipulates her victimhood on page 107.

Activity: Invent a character simply by listing the clothes and accessories they have. What does this show you about your character? Give the list to your classmate and see if they can tell you about the character's personality just from this list.

Activity: Think about the clothes in your own wardrobe. Do you wear different kinds of clothes for different occasions or to give a certain impression? Draw an outfit as if you were going to a wedding, then to school, then if you are staying at home for the day. What clothes have you picked for each occasion?

Izzy

Izzy is the protagonist of the story. Most protagonists change over the course of their adventure, or show character growth. The explanation for Izzy's dreams and the resolution of *The Mystery of the Colour Thief* are revealed on page 163. In the following chapter, on page 165, Frank says that Izzy looks different.

Discuss: Why might that be? How has Izzy grown during the course of the novel? To help you, look at when Lou says that Izzy has nothing to look forward to on page 76, but on page 95, Izzy says 'I was already looking forward to coming back again tomorrow.' What has helped Izzy to change her mindset?

Activity: In order to be happy, it is important to have things to look forward to. Make a list of things you are looking forward to. It might be something small like a meal or particular food or TV programme, or it might be something big, such as a holiday.

Lou

From the beginning of the novel it's very clear that Izzy and Lou's friendship has broken down:

'Lou saw me by the lockers and gave me a disapproving glance, not mentioning a word about why she hadn't come to mine. I'd got used to these glances over the last few weeks. Ever since we'd started Year Eight, she'd been acting as though she was a guru on everything from clothes to hair, music and even who to hang around with' (page 3). The reader only sees their friendship from Izzy's point of view.

Activity: What kind of person do you think Lou is? Can you write either a diary entry for the first day of school from Lou's point of view, or write a letter from Lou to Izzy, explaining why the friendship isn't working.

Look at the end of Chapter One, on page 7. 'We'd been friends since playschool. She wouldn't give up on me. Would she?'

Discuss: What does the author mean by this? What emotions does it convey? And why do you think the author chooses to end the first chapter with a question?

'Now that I noticed them sitting together, speaking in hushed whispers, I could see the similarities between her [Jemima] and Lou. They'd practically merged into each other with their high-heeled polished shoes, sheets of poker-straight hair and mocking expressions. They even had the same phone covers in a leopard print pattern' (page 74).

'She's a loser anyway - it's the only thing she has to look forward to' (page 76).

Discuss: Why do you think Lou says such unkind words about her former friend to Jemima?

Toby

Look at how the author introduces Toby: 'a small silhouetted figure. At first I thought it might be a person sitting on a chair, which struck me as a strange thing to be doing in the middle of the pavement, but as I got closer, I saw it was a wheelchair.

In it sat a boy of about my age, with blond hair. A pair of round glasses balanced on his upturned nose. He grinned and waved. Just like that. It was the weirdest thing' (page 15).

Discuss: What are your first impressions of Toby? Think about the fact that Izzy first notices his chair. What must it be like in Toby's situation? Think about the things Toby could do before his accident, and the things he can do afterwards. (For reference on the accident, see pages 128-129.)

Activity: Write two lists, before and after activities. Compare with your friends.

Now read again from page 15 to page 17 when Toby gives his name.

Discuss: Write down your further impressions of Toby.

Toby and Izzy quickly become good friends.

Activity: What does it mean to be a good friend? Can you write a list of attributes a good friend should have? And then put ticks by the ones you think Toby demonstrates in the book.

Izzy's dad

'Dad was lying, still in his work clothes, on top of the duvet. There was a stack of papers next to him, some on the pillow; others had slipped on to the floor. I sat on the edge of the bed and took hold of his shoulders' (page 28).

Discuss: Izzy's dad is also suffering from the effects of the accident and how it left her mother. What clues can you find in the text that everything isn't okay with him? Is he a good dad? Think about when he is, and when he isn't. Look carefully at pages 103-104 as well. What clues is the author giving about Izzy's dad here?

Themes

Animals and Nature

For much of the novel, Izzy and Toby take care of the smallest cygnet - the baby swan they name Spike. Toby looks up facts about cygnets to help take care of him. See page 48 for Toby's research on swans.

Activity: Can you make an information poster about swans and cygnets? Think about their habitat, feeding habits, life cycle. Use the book to help you and then do some further research online.

Izzy's dad is also very interested in caring for animals. He has started a company called Project Elephant to help save elephants from poaching (page 29).

Discuss: What do you think the author's viewpoint on poaching is? How does Izzy's father's job reflect the sort of person he is?

Activity: Do some research on the Internet. What can you find out about poaching? You might want to start here: *http://www.bbc.co.uk/newsround/37373034*

Can you make a leaflet to prevent people from poaching. Which images will you show? What persuasive language can you use?

Izzy loves her dog Milo very much, but there is some imagery in the book that uses animals in a scary way. Think about why the author uses insects to represent fear or anxiety. Izzy is often described as having 'spiders scuttling' when she feels uneasy: 'I felt a spidery scuttling through my stomach...' (page 27), and 'the spiders stomped, moving from my stomach to my chest, leaving a horrible tickling ache' (page 36).

Discuss: Think about how the author uses animals as both a comfort and as a way to represent fear in the book. Do you find animals comforting? And how do you express fear or anxiety? Do you understand what she means by the scuttling in her stomach?

Activity: Write an A-Z of feelings and then write an animal that symbolises that feeling next to it. Add a third column and put a part of the body in which you feel that feeling, e.g. you might feel butterflies in your stomach for nervousness, you might feel that a dog represents love, and you might feel the sensation in your chest.

Colour

Ewa Jozefkowicz uses colour in the novel to indicate mood. Look at the 'autumn leaves, clusters of reds and oranges' (page 85), or 'the human body is quite literally filled with colour' (page 88), and how she uses red in different ways - as anger, as red blood cells, as the colour to show Spike his house from far away.

Discuss: Why does Izzy call the day of her Mum's accident 'the Blackest Day' (page 28)? What does the colour black represent here? If you have a bad day, which colour would you attribute to it and why? What colour would you paint your bedroom if you could? Why?

Activity: Investigate how we see colour. This link may help you: *https://www.bbc.co.uk/education/guides/zq7thyc/revision/6*

Activity: Make a Newton Colour Wheel. This link may help you: *http://www.planet-science.com/categories/experiments/magic-tricks/2010/12/can-you-make-a-rainbow-disappear.aspx* Spin the wheel fast to see the colours disappear. Read about why this happens.

In *The Mystery of the Colour Thief*, colour reflects how people are feeling. At the start of the novel, Izzy worries that she'll be 'bland and boring... and grey' on stage (page 63). By the end of the book, Izzy says 'I no longer felt bland and grey - I felt coloured in, in full technicolour...' (page 174).

Discuss: What does she mean by that?

Art and Drama

When Izzy's mum was four, she started painting a mural on Izzy's bedroom wall showing key moments from Izzy's life in squares (page 26).

Activity: Using a comic book style, try drawing a few key moments from your life. What have you chosen? What do these moments show? Who are the other characters that appear in your comic strip? In the book, the colours on the mural are very important to

Izzy. What colours have you used? What colour are you wearing in the pictures? Think carefully about what your colours represent.

Izzy auditions for the role of Lady Macbeth in Shakespeare's *Macbeth*.

Activity: What can you find out about the story of *Macbeth*? *https://www.bbc.co.uk/education/clips/zgd4qty*

'Lady Macbeth and I. We had both done something terrible, something truly bad. And what was more, we were being punished for it' (page 75).

Discuss: What does the author mean by this?

Activity: Can you think of a book character similar to you, or to whom you feel a connection? Can you write a couple of paragraphs explaining why?

In the end, Izzy realises that she's nothing like Lady Macbeth. 'She had deliberately gone out to hurt people, and that wasn't me at all' (page 174). Now explain the ways in which you are different to the character you have chosen.

One of the key themes in *Macbeth* is 'appearances' - whether things are real or not. Lady Macbeth imagines blood on her hands. This is a symbol of her guilt.

Discuss: Think about Izzy's guilt in the book - what does she feel guilty about? Is she justified in this?

What symbolises Izzy's guilt in the story? Look at the following sentence about things seen and unseen: 'And I remained the only person who could see what the colour thief had stolen, which simply meant that it wasn't real' (page 132). Why do you think the author wrote this?

Toby suggests to Izzy that sometimes he imagines doing a life swap with somebody, so that you know what it's like to walk in somebody else's shoes. Izzy relates to this because it's like acting.

Activity: Can you think of someone you'd like to be for an hour or a day? Why would you want to swap with them? Write a description of how you see the world from their eyes. It could be a celebrity, or someone you know in your own life.

Guilt

'It was a good question. There was so much I was sorry for that I was bursting with it. And even if I tried to put it into words for Dad, I knew I wouldn't be able to' (page 101).

Izzy feels guilt in the story, both for her mother's accident, but also for what she does to Lou: 'I tried to catch Lou's eye and eventually she looked up at me. Her face was still flushed. She looked scared, and I felt awful. I mouthed the words "I'm sorry," but she deliberately turned away' (page 79). Izzy also apologises to her mother in a coma (page 13).

Discuss: Is Izzy right to feel guilty about her mother's accident? Is Izzy right to feel guilty about what she did to Lou? Think about something you have felt sorry about, and whether your apology was accepted. How did it make you feel? Have you ever not accepted an apology? Why?

The headmistress tells her not to be sorry. Izzy is surprised by this (page 81).

Discuss: Were you surprised when you read it? What does the headmistress mean? Why does Izzy want the headmistress to yell at her instead?

Discuss: What is the difference between being sorry and feeling sorry for someone? Think about the word. What is the difference between regret and guilt? Why do we apologise?

Activity: Make a list of apologising phrases, and then make a list of accepting an apology phrases. Roleplay them with your classmate. Which works best? Which sounds most sincere?

Independence and When to Ask for Help

When Izzy makes friends with Toby, she is surprised to find how fiercely independent he is: 'At the base of the riverbank, his wheelchair lodged itself in the mud, and I rushed to help, but once again, he'd already extracted himself before I got there' (page 22).

Discuss: Why do you think Toby wants to be so independent?

'No one else would understand about the colour thief' (page 36).

Discuss: Why do you think Izzy thinks that? Is she right or wrong? If you have nightmares, is it worth sharing them with a trusted adult or friend? Izzy thinks only she will notice the colours have gone. What is the author trying to do here?

'He smiled sadly and turned his gaze in the direction of the mural. I waited for him to say something, but his expression didn't change. It was obvious he couldn't see that the colours had disappeared. I felt lonelier than ever' (page 69).

Discuss: Do you think that Izzy's dad can't see the colours have disappeared, or do you think he too doesn't want to admit it? Explain your reasoning.

Activity: Sometimes it's hard to talk about something that's upsetting you, but usually a trouble shared is easier to fix. Can you think of when it was hard to share something? How else might you express what's upsetting you? Izzy uses art and drama as ways to express herself. Think of advice you could offer your friend if something was troubling them but they couldn't tell you how. Brainstorm a mind map of ideas on how to express your troubles, e.g. art, music, diary writing etc.

Read pages 90-92 again. Izzy says 'sometimes I feel like I can't really do anything - I can't change anything.'

Discuss: Why does Izzy feel powerless?

Activity: Think about the changes you can effect and the things you can't. Have you ever felt frustrated about something and wondered how you could make a difference? Choose a cause you believe in and draw up a plan for how to effect change. This could be a global issue, a local issue or even a personal issue. What methods could you use? A petition, or writing a letter to an MP. Have you ever joined a protest march? Write a list of ways you could make a difference to causes you care about. If it's a personal cause, could you write a letter to someone, make a speech, even just start a conversation?

Later in the novel, Toby asks for help: 'I was surprised when he said: "Could you give me a hand?"' (page 136).

Discuss: Why is Izzy surprised? Why does it take so long for Toby to ask her for help directly?

Activity: Toby confides in Izzy about his own disability and accident, what he can do and what he can't. Create a Mind Map. Write your name in the middle of a piece of paper, then around you draw lines to your own support network - the people around you in whom you can confide. Think about what you can share with each person. Is it different? How do they help you? Are they peers/friends/family or adults in authority?

Look at the author's comparisons between Spike and Toby, and even Izzy: 'He seemed somehow more solid than before. He'd grown, and his feathers were less fluffy. He flexed his wings slightly, reminding me that one day, of course, he would be able to fly. He no longer seemed as if he would be blown away in a single gust' (page 139), and:

'"He was weak," Toby answered. "But you can't automatically assume he won't make it." He sounded mad' (page 90).

Discuss: Why is Toby mad? Think about what Spike might represent? How does Toby identify with Spike? Is Spike like Toby or even like Izzy? Does a person's independence change how you view them?

When Spike grows, Izzy explains: 'He's been through a lot of change, and now he has so many amazing possibilities before him. He can go anywhere he wants' (page 142).

Activity: Look up the story of *The Ugly Duckling*. Explore how the story relates to the story of Izzy.

'But then it turns out that you're stronger than you think. And sometimes you just need a bit of help' (page 171).

Discuss: Izzy says this to her mother, about her mother. But is she really talking about her mother? Think about when in the novel Izzy needs help, and when she accepts it. Think about situations in which you need help. Do you ask for help in all these situations? Explore why.

Memory and Time

Things fading is a large theme within the book. Izzy's mural that documents key moments in her life seems to be fading as the colours ebb away. But then she looks at her father's mug in the kitchen and the colours on that have faded too - but for a different reason (page 37).

Discuss: When do things fade? Do physical things fade from overuse? Does memory fade as it becomes more distant? Think about the colour draining from people's faces when they are ill. What does this fading indicate?

When Izzy looks at the display in the history corridor at school, she sees that the colour in the recent pictures of the Year Nine trip to Egypt has faded, making them look more like the older black and white pictures (page 41).

Discuss: Is time a colour thief?

Izzy studies Dalí's *The Persistence of Memory* in art (page 68).

Activity: Take a closer look at the painting:
https://www.moma.org/learn/moma_learning/1168-2

Discuss: How has Dalí used insects in the picture? What do you think they represent?

Dalí was interested in the relationship between actual time and remembered time, and represents this in the melting of the many clocks. Einstein said that 'time is relative'. 'Time swung suspended at night; it didn't leak away at its normal speed' (page 151).

Discuss: What do the clocks in the painting represent to you? Think about how you use time. When does it go quickly and when slowly?

'Dreams and clocks were linked to the colour thief. He'd appeared first in a dream, which was really more of a nightmare, and when he'd faded from my mind, the first things I always saw were the luminous numerals on my clock' (page 46-47).

Discuss: Why is time so important to Izzy? Why does she think of her aunt as an old-fashioned watchmaker (page 57)?

'Dalí often described his paintings as "hand-painted dream photographs", he said' (page 109).

Discuss: What is meant by hand-painted dream photograph? Look at the words 'dream' and photograph next to each other. Is this a contradiction in terms? If a photograph is a true representation of fact, is a dream a fiction?

Izzy's dad interprets the painting: 'It's because sometimes your memories are constantly with you, whether you want them to be or not. Time passes, the clocks move on, but you remain stuck there - your useless, floppy clock always telling the same time. And even if you think you've escaped, your memories always catch up with you' (page 68).

Discuss: What does he mean by this? Are your memories constantly with you?

Look at pages 98-99. Izzy has a memory of her skiing from when she was quite young, but there's a piece of the memory she can't picture, and she has to get her father to help her solve the mystery.

Activity: Think back to a childhood memory and try to write about it. Then go and ask a parent or carer about that memory. Do they remember it differently? Think about how they saw that time from their point of view. Has their memory distorted yours or made you feel differently about it?

Towards the end of the novel, Toby shows Izzy his 'Before Box' (page 136). Note how it contains feathers of different colours. But also, think about how it captures memories with mementos and pictures.

Activity: If you were making a box about the previous year of your life, what would you put in it? Find an old shoe box and see if you can decorate it stating the year, then fill it with small bits and pieces that remind you of the past year. Attach a small label to each one explaining your reason for it being there.

Language Questions

Discuss: Did you find the book easy to read? Explore your reasons why.

Look at the first chapter again. Explore the different ways the author starts her sentences, the variety of length of sentence, and the amount of dialogue.

Activity: Highlight when Izzy uses her different senses in the first chapter. When does she 'hear' something, 'see' something, 'feel' something? Are there smells and tastes? Think about how the author makes you feel emotion.

Vocabulary

Izzy's dad likes to make up words using a fusion of other words, for example 'specsational', which is a mixture of spectacular and sensational.

Activity: Can you have a go at making up a list of ten new words from a combination of other words?

© Clare Zinkin, Children's Reading Consultant

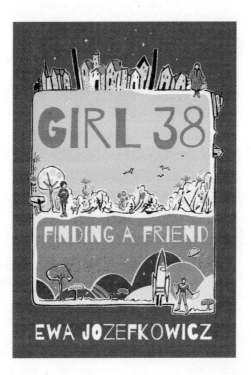

Now enjoy reading the first chapter
of *Girl 38: Finding a Friend*

ONE

Captain Eagle Heart had done all he could, but everyone on board could hear the engine struggling. An ear-splitting screech ripped the air. Some of the crew started to scream, waiting for the crash, but Girl 38 knew that they were going to make it. She wasn't like the other girls. She was a highly-skilled space-traveller – cool-headed, noble and brave —

'Kat, what are you doing? Drawing that stupid comic again? Look…' Gem hissed at me. 'He's here. Apparently he has some news for us. I overheard him talking to Miss Seymour in the corridor.'

I added the finishing touches to crazy, fiery sparks exploding from the spacecraft before I looked up and saw Mr Kim strolling into the classroom. I immediately felt my face heat up. I'd forgotten how tall he was – he looked like one of those celebrity basketball players. He'd had a haircut over the holidays and got different glasses.

I glanced at my sketch of Captain Eagle Heart and regretted getting so far ahead with it. He was modelled on Mr Kim, and I could now see that his new look suited the character much better. But then again, maybe it was for the best. Gem would have definitely noticed the similarity and I wouldn't have heard the end of it.

'Greetings, all,' he said to us, giving an exaggerated wave. I heard Gem sigh. Unlike me, she didn't think much of him, but then sometimes I wondered whether she thought much of anyone apart from Arun.

'Welcome to a new term. I hope you all had a great six weeks off. I'm sure you have some wonderful stories to tell. Save them until lunchtime if you possibly can though, because I need to take the register and then I have an important announcement.'

I could tell that Gem was distracted – something, or rather someone, across the room had caught her eye. She whispered from behind her long, dark hair, 'I'm going to go on a date with him this term.'

For a second I thought she meant Mr Kim and I wondered if she'd lost the plot, but she was gazing at Arun, who was busy looking at his phone under the desk.

'What? Seriously?' I asked her.

'Yeah, my horoscope said so. It'll probably happen in September, maybe October at the latest.'

'Right.' I didn't know what else to say.

'Gemma, I'm sure you're not listening,' Mr Kim said. 'And if you *were* listening, you might find that you're interested. As I was saying, Julius will be joining us tomorrow. His family are still in the process of moving, so unfortunately he couldn't make it in today. But I want you all to make him feel welcome when he starts. He's a top swimmer and he comes from a fascinating part of the country, so he'll have loads to tell you. Now… next on my list – your timetables.'

A red spot appeared high up on Gem's cheek. She'd always had that spot. The first time I'd noticed it was when we were in nursery and there was a prize for the most helpful person in our class. It went to a girl called Molly. Gem didn't cry or anything – I just saw the red spot appear and then her fists clenched tightly at her sides. My own stomach knotted with nerves when I saw it. I guessed that, right now, she was already prickling at the thought of Julius maybe being better than her at swimming, perhaps other things too. It was unlikely, of course, as Gem's the swimming champion, and best in our class at most things. Even so, she doesn't like anyone or anything that might be a threat.

I've known Gem since we were three, which is a super long time – over nine years. We met at the gates of nursery on our first day there. She was shorter than me and wore a big fluffy white dress that made her look a bit like a snowman.

'Want to be my friend?' she'd asked.

I'd nodded. It was as simple as that. I thought I was lucky, because there were always a lot of people who wanted to be Gem's friend, but she only chose me. And she looked out for me after that. If you weren't Gem's friend then you fell into a category of people who she could, at any moment, decide were her enemies. It wasn't good to get on the wrong side of her.

Throughout primary school it had always been the two of us. We sat next to each other in all our lessons, we were always partners in any activities and we were round at each other's houses most nights.

Dad seemed to think that I could do with mixing in a bigger crowd, but I told him that I didn't need to. I had Gem.

Then, at the end of Year Six, there was a panic, as

Mum and Dad wanted me to go to the Castle School, which is a private girls' school in town. Two sisters, Maisie and Abigail, on my street go there. They wear uniforms with long, pleated skirts and they sound posh. I wouldn't go, of course, unless Gem did, and it turned out that her mum would never have been able to afford it – not with four other children. It wouldn't have been fair if she'd only sent Gem.

'I don't care!' Gem shouted at me when she found out that her mum wouldn't even agree to them going to look round on an open day. 'I don't want to go there anyway. You sit in your lah-di-dah castle while the rest of us carry on here in the real world. I knew you were stuck up! It's always about you and nobody else.'

None of that was true, especially not the last part. In fact, I was always thinking about Gem. I cried and cried. I was scared of losing her. I begged my parents not to send me to 'the stupid castle'. I got myself into such a state that I made myself ill. In the end, unbelievably, they gave in and I went to Marley High with Gem and most of the others from our primary school class.

Of course, I thought that it would be the same as ever – me and her – but, no. Gem decided that she needed a bigger gang. First, she made friends with

Ruby, a tall, thin girl with pale brown skin and her hair done in hundreds of little plaits. Then Ruby introduced her to Dilly, who was round-faced and ginger, and super enthusiastic about everything. So our two became a four and things weren't the same after that.

I still sit next to Gem but we don't do anything just the two of us anymore. Ruby and Dilly are always there. It's not that I don't like them, but it seems like most of the things they do are to impress Gem or to make her laugh. Guess I do that too. If they don't succeed, they're miserable for the rest of the day.

Today, Gem gathered the three of us round her at lunch and asked casually, 'This Julius. What d'you reckon?'

'Sounds like a Vilk to me.'

Ruby and Dil looked confused, but Gem knew what I meant. It was our private joke; the Vilks were the enemy in *Girl 38*, which I'd only shown to her. But she didn't laugh like I thought she would.

'He might be all right,' Gem said, pretending for a second to be cool about it. 'Who knows? Maybe he'll create a bit of excitement. Our class is so *boring* these days.'

When she said that, I wondered for a moment if

she meant me, and I felt a tingling of nerves in my stomach. I had a strange intuition that this new guy was about to change everything.

Zephyr is an imprint of Head of Zeus.
At Zephyr we are proud to publish books you can
read and re-read time and time again because they tell
a brilliant story and because they entertain you.

Subscribe to our newsletter to hear all the latest news
about upcoming releases, competitions and to have the
chance to win signed books. Just drop us a line at
hello@headofzeus.com.

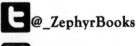 @_ZephyrBooks

HeadofZeus

www.readzephyr.com

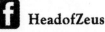 ZEPHYR